She pressed h
mirrored her action.

Oh no.

First the possible flirting, and now this. She wanted to kiss him—there was no point lying to herself.

He wants to kiss you too.

And so what if he did?

Nothing. Absolutely nothing. Leaning into this moment would be a very bad decision indeed.

"Thanks again for a lovely evening and for showing me the village, and the pub."

Henry reached out his right hand, but a look of confusion crossed his face and he dropped it again. He looked as conflicted as she felt and she wanted to laugh out loud, but held her giggle back.

He lifted his hand again and held it out for a shake. She took it. It should have been a perfectly formal gesture, but when his hand enclosed hers, it was nothing of the sort. Warm, secure tingles shot up her arm and directly into her heart. His hand was rougher than hers but his grip was tender. She felt her insides melting.

Henry leaned forward, just the merest of fractions, just enough to make her heart leap into her throat, but then he drew back.

"Good night, Laura." His voice was rough and low and it rippled through her insides, reaching every long-forgotten crevice and hole.

Dear Reader,

This book does have many swoony scenes, baby animals, sexy moments and of course a satisfying HEA, but it also deals with infertility. I've tried to write about it as sensitively as possible and hope I've succeeded, but I also understand that it isn't a topic everyone wants to read about at every stage of their lives. I wanted to let you know before you dive in.

Take care and look after yourselves,

Justine

xx

SWIPE RIGHT FOR MR. PERFECT

JUSTINE LEWIS

H Harlequin
ROMANCE

Harlequin®
ROMANCE

ISBN-13: 978-1-335-21616-8

Swipe Right for Mr. Perfect

Recycling programs for this product may not exist in your area.

Harlequin Enterprises ULC
22 Adelaide St. West, 41st Floor
Toronto, Ontario M5H 4E3, Canada
www.Harlequin.com

Printed in U.S.A.

Justine Lewis writes uplifting, heartwarming contemporary romances. She lives in Australia with her hero husband, two teenagers and an outgoing puppy. When she isn't writing, she loves to walk her dog in the bush near her house, attempt to keep her garden alive and search for the perfect frock. She loves hearing from readers, and you can visit her at justinelewis.com.

Visit the Author Profile page at Harlequin.com.

For Eleanor and Melinda

To cocktails, chats about dating and
Catfish Princesses.

Praise for
Justine Lewis

CHAPTER ONE

LAURA HIT SEND on the condition report she had just prepared for a client on one of their paintings and stretched her arms high into the air. Outside, the London air was warm and the sky still bright as the city shook off winter and the evenings stretched on a little longer. Laura loved that she'd be walking home in daylight; the prospect buoyed her. It had been a long winter, one that had felt particularly dark given the pain she'd been in, and being bedridden following her last laparoscopy, which had taken her longer to recover from than usual.

The offices of the art conservation firm where she worked were not too far from her flat. Laura was glad to be up and moving again and, for the moment at least, able to enjoy the beautiful weather. Before packing and leaving for the day she checked her phone and smiled. There was already a message.

@FarmerDan: How was your lunch?

Laura replied as the online alias she used on the dating app.

@SohoJane: Lunch was delicious, my mother on the other hand...

@FarmerDan: Not so tasty?

@SohoJane: Ha-ha. You'd like her. You'd both have at least one thing in common. You both want me to meet you.

Laura stopped before she hit Reply on the last message, deleted most of the words and simply replied with:

@SohoJane: Ha-ha.

@FarmerDan: How was *her* date?

@SohoJane: Which one? She goes on more dates than either of us.

@FarmerDan: The one with the guy you think did time?

@SohoJane: Oh, him. Yes, he wasn't an ex-crim just an ex-local councillor.

@FarmerDan: Fair enough. Is she seeing him again?

@SohoJane: No, there are too many better prospects apparently. The sixty-plus dating pool is where all the action is at.

Was it normal to talk so much about your mother with a guy you'd never even met? Laura shut down her computer, bid good evening to her colleagues, a close group of like-minded people who shared her passion for art and conservation and who had been amazingly supportive through the last few years of her life. Outside, the air was even warmer than she imagined. The temperature in their offices was kept constant to ensure the pieces they worked on were not further damaged. They did a lot of their work in their London studio, but also travelled frequently to their clients. As she walked across Hyde Park, marvelling at the number of people who had come out to enjoy the evening, she kept messaging Dan. It had become an early evening ritual for both of them to check in with one another at this time of day. Sometimes it was just a brief chat, other times their conversation would stretch on into the night.

@FarmerDan: Your mum could write the book

on online dating. There's definitely a market for Fiona's dating wisdom.

Laura grimaced. He was probably right. Laura's father passed away nearly a decade ago. Fiona had struggled for many years after losing her husband, but the passage of time had eased her grief and Fiona had launched herself into her sixties and recent retirement with gusto. She called it her 'Finaissance' and had thrown herself back into the world: dating, learning photography, volunteering and travelling. Her mother's activities exhausted Laura but fascinated Dan.

@SohoJane: Yes, but you're not her daughter.

Fiona had a lot to say on the topic of online dating, and dating in general, though Laura was not in the right space to be receiving her mother's particular brand of advice at this point in time.

Laura had been messaging Dan casually on a dating app for a few weeks when she'd had a particularly devastating discussion with her doctor about her fertility status and future treatment options. She had told Dan she was stepping away from dating for a bit, but Dan had written back wishing her the best. Somehow they hadn't stopped messaging. Their conversations had been much more honest from that point on, as well.

Once a relationship was taken off the table they both seemed to speak more openly, about life and in particular, dating. Dan would tell her about his dates and online dating disasters and she shared her mother's escapades.

Since then, Laura had had further surgery in an attempt to relieve her symptoms. After a terrible start, she was beginning to feel well. She was cautiously hopeful. She had to be. If this didn't work there were few other options left, apart from the most radical of all. A hysterectomy.

Dr Healy, who had been treating Laura for endometriosis for a decade, since her early twenties, said she almost never resorted to those steps in women who had not had children.

'Almost never?' Laura had questioned. 'What does that mean?'

'I mean, it's not a decision you make until we've tried everything else.'

Laura wasn't even sure if she wanted children; it was something she'd never really allowed herself to contemplate, knowing as she always had that it would likely be more difficult for her. Her main priority over the years had been trying to be pain free enough to live a full life.

Over the past few months, chatting with a farmer from Gloucestershire, a man she should have nothing in common with but appeared to have everything in common with, was a kind of solace. Most of her friends and colleagues knew about her condition—they had to. Her frequent absences from work, her need to cancel dates when her symptoms were too bad, made concealing her condition from people close to her impossible.

But Dan didn't know anything and that was freeing.

While she was laid up at home his messages were the bright point of her day. All her friends and workmates wrote to her with sympathetic questions about how she was doing, but Dan was oblivious to everything else going on in her life and she liked that. She liked having someone who was not part of her world.

He didn't constantly ask her how she was. How she'd been. Didn't ask for a pain status update. He just chatted. About everything and sometimes nothing.

Would you rather drink coffee or tea for the rest of your life?

Tea, though just writing that makes me long for my morning latte. You?

It would be an impossible choice, but I'd say coffee.

Would you rather be attacked by a shark or a crocodile?

Is neither an option?

Apart from silly quizzes, she told him about

her job as an art conservator. Usually once a new acquaintance had asked what her job involved the questions ended, but Dan had plenty more: What do you love about it? What era do you specialise in? Who are your favourite artists? She couldn't resist talking about her work. What did she love about it? Everything! She loved the science, the problem solving, the history and most of all making sure that beautiful and important works of art survived for generations to come.

In turn, she asked about his work. Why had he become a farmer?

@FarmerDan: Family business, I'm afraid.

@SohoJane: You're afraid? Did you not want to be a farmer?

@FarmerDan: No, I did. I do. I'm happy to do it. I love it.

Something about his choice of words indicated a level of hesitancy, but Laura let it go.

@SohoJane: What do you like about it?

@FarmerDan: Many things! The animals. Being outside. And it probably sounds corny, but I like the satisfaction you get by helping things grow.

She didn't think that was corny at all. It made her smile. Dan often made her smile. He seemed like a lovely, down-to-earth man. So different from many of the other men she met in London. Maybe she should listen to her mother's advice and meet him already.

No. She stopped that thought there. She and Dan worked well as friends. And she wasn't going to date anyone until she had a better idea about her condition and her next steps.

But they kept chatting. About life in general. They both had mothers who were very keen to see them settled. Dan's mother was a greater meddler even than Fiona, going so far as to invite single women along to occasions when Dan was expecting a lunch or dinner alone with his mother.

Laura knew their friendship had moved on from potential partners to friends when Dan started mentioning some dates he'd been on. At first Laura had a pang of sadness, but then quickly reminded herself that not only was she the one to say she didn't want a relationship, but that she actually *didn't* want a relationship. Not at this point in her life anyway.

At home, Laura sat on the couch in her small apartment, eating a sandwich she had been too distracted to eat at lunchtime and messages bounced between them.

A Deux was an exclusive app. Exclusive and

expensive. The cost had given her pause, but she paid the money to have her identity protected and to know that the users of the app had been vetted first. By an actual person, not an algorithm.

Many of the users revealed everything about themselves—there were some celebrities who were very keen for everyone to know who they were—but just as many users remained anonymous, or partially anonymous, like Laura. The app had allowed her not to worry that the person she was chatting with was a scammer. Or a stalker. Laura had been burnt before by a man who had created fake profiles to keep chatting with her once their brief relationship had ended. Despite reporting him to the managers of the app, he kept finding ways to reach her. She had almost given up online dating entirely at that point, until her mother had told her about A Deux.

Laura didn't use her real name, and while her profile picture showed her face, it was in black-and-white and didn't expose every pore. She wasn't unrecognisable to someone who knew her well but was anonymous enough she wouldn't be spotted by an acquaintance. She hadn't had nearly as many matches as she did on other apps, but A Deux promised to keep its clients safe and kicked off anyone about whom a complaint had been made.

As an unexpected bonus, Laura wasn't on the

same site as her mother. She loved her mother, but dating alongside her was strange. Fiona knew about Laura's friendship with Dan and had gently been encouraging her to meet him, even just as friends. '*A trip out of London would do you good,*' Fiona had suggested.

Meanwhile, Dan had let it slip that he did spend some time in London to visit his mother and 'do business.' Laura wasn't exactly sure what visiting London entailed for a farmer.

A farmer. She'd never known any farmers and couldn't quite get her head around what he did each day, but she was curious to know. And dating stockbrokers and lawyers hadn't exactly worked out for her so she was open to anything.

But you aren't dating Dan. You're just chatting.

The next morning broke bright and clear again. Each day that was pain free filled Laura with hope. It was wonderful to be able to go so long without spending a day at home, curled up in bed. She was planning on continuing an assessment of a John Everett Millais painting. Working on a painting she'd known and loved for years was exhilarating, but also an honour.

'Laura, good news. They signed off on your trip to Abney Castle.'

Laura took off the magnifying glasses and

torch with which she was assessing the canvas and refocused her gaze on her supervisor, Brett.

'You're going to Gloucestershire next week.'

Laura's mentor, Archibald Peterson, had been the conservator requested by Abney Castle for years, even when he was meant to be retired. He loved the collection so much and the family was so fond of him, he visited them biannually, as long as his health permitted. Before he'd passed away he'd recommended Laura take over for him and, much to Laura's delight, the family had taken his recommendation. It included an important and thoughtfully assembled collection of eighteenth- and nineteenth-century British art, including many by Laura's favourite artist, J. M. W. Turner.

It was a wonderful opportunity, and further evidence that something was turning around in her life.

'Great! I'll book my accommodation.'

'No need. They've said you can stay there.'

'At the castle?'

'Well, in the servants' quarters anyway. There's a cottage you can use.'

'Really?'

'Yes, really. You'll have all the privacy you need. But if you'd rather stay at a B & B in the village, you can.'

'I'm sure the cottage will be fine.'

Archibald had visited Abney Castle regularly

for as long as she'd known him and come back
with stories about how welcoming the elderly
Duke and Duchess of Brighton were, even invit-
ing him to join them for meals on occasion. While
she doubted she'd obtain the same degree of inti-
macy Archibald had, she hoped she wouldn't let
them, or Archibald, down.

Back at her desk, Laura googled Abney Castle
and gasped. She was familiar with the paintings
in the Duke of Brighton's collection, but not his
seat of Abney Castle. England being England, the
Duke of Brighton was based in Gloucestershire,
nowhere near Brighton.

The website showed that Abney Castle was still
privately owned, but opened to tourists six days
a week. The castle was a Grade I–listed property
and had been owned by the Dukes of Brighton
for over four hundred years. It was also a func-
tioning organic farm, with an animal nursery and
cider distillery. The photos of the grounds made
her breath catch. The place was gorgeous. And it
would be her home for the next few weeks.

There was also a photo of the duke and his
duchess. They were seated, straight backed, in an
opulent room. He in particular looked frail, but
both held friendly smiles. She hoped they were really as kind as they appeared in their photograph.
While clients generally treated their conservators
well, everyone had at least one bad story about a

client who had unrealistic expectations. Laura's job was primarily to protect the art works from further degeneration—she cleaned the paintings and suggested steps for further care—but it was rare to recommend attempting to restore the art to its original condition. As conservators, they did not do anything to the artwork that was not reversible.

The job at Abney was significant. Several hundred paintings, some particularly large. The paintings would have been well looked after under Archibald's care, and assessed very regularly, which allayed most of her concerns. But it was a big job. She'd be away for several weeks. What if she became ill during her visit?

She closed the browser.

She was going to Abney Castle. For a few glorious weeks she would escape her mother's interrogation, concentrate on her work and have space to figure out her next steps. And if she got sick, she'd manage. She always had before.

She might even meet a real-life duke.

That evening Laura met two girlfriends for a drink on the way home. It was later than usual by the time she finally connected with Dan.

@FarmerDan: How was your day? Best thing? Worst thing?

She loved that he took the time to ask this, it was like her father had once done when she was a child. The memory of her father was bittersweet; if she hadn't had a wonderful childhood then his loss wouldn't hurt so much.

@SohoJane: Worst thing was the coffee. We tried a new place and urgh. Won't be going back. But that probably means I had a pretty good day.

@FarmerDan: So the best thing?

@SohoJane: A career highlight, I think.

@FarmerDan: Amazing, congratulations. Do tell!

Laura stared at her phone. Even if Dan was unlikely to say anything, she doubted the duke and duchess would be happy with her telling a stranger about her new assignment without their prior approval. She knew her firm would certainly not be. They had very strict policies around discussing their clients, which included royalty, celebrities and of course the aristocracy. Besides, if she told him what the assignment was and that she'd be staying close to where he lived for a few weeks then she'd feel extra pressure to finally meet him. He wouldn't press her, but it would feel strange to go to his part of the country and not suggest they meet.

@SohoJane: I can't say exactly, but I've been given a very prestigious collection to work on. It's very exciting.

@FarmerDan: Congratulations! I'm sure it's very well deserved because I'm sure you're fabulous at your job.

His absolute confidence in her made her entire chest warm with pride.

Should she tell him she was coming to Gloucestershire? It was hardly a small place, but she'd be closer than she was in London.

No. She'd wait a little.

At times she was overwhelmed with the urge to tell him everything about her, about her life. At times she wanted to call him, longed to hear the sound of his voice, but she had to keep those feelings in check. She had good reasons for holding back.

Henry took off his jacket and slung it over his shoulder as he walked down Piccadilly, towards Hyde Park. It was an unseasonably warm spring day and he was close to concluding the business on one of his monthly trips to London. He'd attended a board meeting of the children's charity of which he was a patron and met with the family accountant. He'd also managed to squeeze in a quick lunch with one of his university friends, but was now, thankfully, making his way back to his house in Mayfair.

His phone buzzed and he looked at it immediately. This was usually the time of day he'd start to expect a message from Jane. He had a self-imposed time of not messaging her before five in the afternoon. His impulse was to send her a brief message first thing in the morning, but he knew that not only would he be coming on too strong, but the rest of the day would be spent messaging with her. Chatting with her was like a compulsion for him; it seemed they had an endless number of things to talk about, especially for a couple who had never met in person.

Henry had almost given up on online dating when his friend suggested A Deux, an exclusive site with people who were vetted by the business owner. Women were attracted to the site because it was considered safer—Henry had been attracted by the idea that he could maintain his anonymity for longer than usual. He liked to get to know someone—and for them to get know him—before meeting in person.

Before they found out he was a duke.

He'd made the mistake of putting his full name, not even his title, on the dating sites before, but not this time. This time he was FarmerDan. He wanted to meet a person who liked him—not his name or his title.

He knew he had to marry, preferably within the next few years, because, and there was no way of getting around it, he needed an heir. In the absence of a direct heir—male or female— the Duchy of Brighton would cease to exist. A four-hundred-year-old title would end with him, the thirteenth duke.

Dukedoms and titles had become extinct in the past, probably not mourned by many people, except their own family. His own family—but particularly his own parents—had made too many sacrifices to preserve the title for Henry to lose it.

Besides, getting married? Having children? Those were both things that Henry longed to do— title or no title. He wanted a family and a woman to love and share his life with.

But so far, finding a woman who loved him, Henry Daniel Weston, not Henry, Duke of Brighton, hadn't happened. And he was beginning to doubt that it would.

Henry was in London for one more night. There wasn't an hour that went by that day, during his meetings, his lunch, his drinks that he hadn't started mentally composing a message to Jane.

Hey, I've just popped down to London for business. Don't suppose you'd fancy catching up for a drink?

But knowing her as he did, he didn't send that message.

She was not looking for a romantic relationship at that point; he didn't know why, but he respected it. Yet even though they both understood their relationship would remain platonic, they hadn't stopped messaging one another. He'd expected her to stop. But she hadn't, so neither had he. Knowing she didn't want a relationship hadn't made him less interested in maintaining a friendship. They understood one another, from nearly the outset, and talking to her was like talking to an old friend.

Back at Brighton House, a five-storey Georgian era townhouse near Grosvenor Square, he slipped off his tie and was just about to take off his shoes when he heard voices from the next room. The door to one of the reception rooms was wide open and he paused. Could he walk past and up the stairs without being noticed?

It was a decision he didn't have to make because his mother called out, 'Henry? Henry, darling? Is that you? Come and join us?'

His heart fell.

He didn't want to be speaking to strangers; he wanted to be messaging Jane.

But he was the thirteenth duke of Brighton and he had two jobs: first to keep the family estate largely intact without running up debt for the next generation. Secondly, produce that next generation.

Henry took a deep breath and made himself smile as he walked into the room. There were perhaps a dozen people mingling around, women of all ages, though he guessed that attractive women in the twenty-five to thirty-five age bracket were over-represented. He went over to his mother, Caroline, and kissed her cheek. 'Mum, good evening.'

'Henry, please join us.'

Even knowing he didn't have a choice, he said, 'Oh, no, I wouldn't want to intrude.'

'Nonsense. We don't mind. The more the merrier.'

'Really, I'm sure I could have nothing to add to your...' He looked around the room. Matchmaking party?

'Book club. I've just started a book club.'

Henry bit back a laugh. His mother was the last person on earth he'd imagine in a book club. A walking club, yes. Anything to do with horses, certainly. Art appreciation, maybe. His mother was cultured, but the type of reading matter by her beside was strictly magazines. In all his thirty years he'd never heard her discuss a book.

'Let me introduce you to everyone.'

Twelve sets of eyes looked up at him from where their owners were perched on the various sofas in the room. There was a decent spread of ages, he had to give his mother that. But how on earth she'd managed to hand pick them all and bring them here under the guise of a book club, and tonight of all nights, he could only begin to guess. But Caroline Weston, the Dowager Duchess of Brighton, was known for her organisational skills and powers of persuasion.

Henry sighed, walked over to the sideboard and poured himself a Scotch. He wasn't going to get a moment to himself anytime soon.

'What book did you read?' he asked as he sat down on the nearest sofa and turned to the first candidate, surrendering himself to the evening.

At least, he thought, Jane is going to get a laugh out of this.

'You're angry,' Caroline said three hours later after she bid the last guest/prospective bride goodbye.

'No, I'm just tired.'

'Did you…that is…' Caroline fussed with the sofa cushions, though they both knew full well their housekeeper would come through in the morning to tidy.

'Did I like any of them?' he asked.

Her expression was so hopeful, so earnest.

'They were all lovely. Smart, attractive, good company.'

Her face fell. 'But?'

'But nothing.' He couldn't explain to his mother what the problem was because he didn't understand it himself.

He knew he had to marry and produce an heir. That was not in dispute, but why, when so many eligible, suitable women came across his path was it so hard to choose one? Probably because he used words such as 'eligible' or 'suitable' to describe his future wife. What he was looking for was 'amazing', 'heart-stopping' or 'soul lifting.'

'I just want you to be happy,' Caroline said.

'I know.'

Henry knew his mother wished for his happiness, but only because she believed marrying one of the suitable women she had invited tonight would lead to his happiness. Marrying a suitable woman and producing an heir was in fact the very reason for his existence. The very reason he'd been born in the first place.

His mother kissed him goodnight and Henry finally kicked off his shoes before flopping back onto the nearest sofa and taking out his phone.

There was a message from Jane waiting for him, asking him how his day was.

@FarmerDan: Send wine. And pity. You will not believe what I just walked into.

@SohoJane: A wall?

@FarmerDan: You're on the right track. My mother just ambushed me with a speed dating event disguised as a book club meeting.

@SohoJane: Wow! That's hard core. We must never introduce our mothers to one another.

@FarmerDan: It would probably cause a fissure in the space-time continuum, such would be their combined power.

@SohoJane: Absolutely and I don't know if we can trust them to use their power for good instead of evil.

He liked how he was with her. He felt funnier with her. Was that possible? Was she laughing at his joke? If he saw her in person, he'd be able to tell. He'd be able to watch her face as he spoke, hear her voice…

He was a fool. He should have continued talking to one of the eligible book clubbers, not be spending his time thinking about how to make a woman who wasn't interested in him laugh.

@SohoJane: You're in London?

His heart began to hammer against his ribs. Jane knew his mother lived here.

Just ask her. It's still early.

It was nine thirty. Late enough for anyone who had to work tomorrow.

@FarmerDan: Yes, I've popped down for a brief visit. I thought about letting you know, but I know how you feel so I didn't.

He sat back, waited.
But she didn't respond.

Two days later Henry still hadn't had a response from SohoJane to his message telling her he was in London. He was particularly glad he hadn't said more than that or asked her to meet, but two days was a long time for her to go without replying.

The damp morning gradually brightened into a warm, dry day. Henry spent the morning driving around the grounds and checking the progress of the calves and the lambs. It was spring and they expected two thousand lambs to be born and maybe three hundred calves. They employed a small team of farmers to oversee the farm, but he liked to help out where he could.

The duchy owned fifteen thousand acres of land, one thousand was farmland under his direct management. He had close to fifty tenants, over thirty tenants in the vicinity alone and the rest on the other ducal properties that were scattered across the country.

Then there was the castle.

Abney Castle, the seat of the Dukes of Brighton, was picturesque, but like anything that was several centuries old, it needed constant upkeep and regular health checks. Not to mention a significant budget to pay for them. Opening the castle to the public went some way to paying for its upkeep, but it brought other challenges as well—additional staff, operating costs and further maintenance.

He was fortunate that his father and grandfather had also been good managers and the bulk of their estates was in good order giving them a large buffer for the future, should disaster occur.

Later in the afternoon he had a teleconference with the conservation firm in London about the replacement conservator they were sending. Archibald, the man who had been visiting the estates for the past thirty years, had recently passed away, but they assured him they would send a highly experienced replacement to assess the art collection that his family had collected over the centuries.

The art collection at Abney Castle consisted of over five hundred paintings. From old masters to a significant collection of nineteenth-century British art, including Turner and the Pre-Raphaelites. The entire collection, some of which was lent to the National Gallery and the Tate, numbered in the thousands. The art collection was particularly special; his ancestors had had not only good taste and judgement but exceptional foresight.

Henry meant to see the buildings and the art collections housed inside them protected for generations to come. Other aristocratic families had sold off parts of their collections to fund maintenance of the rest of the estates, but Henry, like his father, saw this as a failure of his management. The estate needed to be maintained, protected and passed down to the next generation. He was only the temporary caretaker of his family's legacy. If anything, he wanted to be in the position of adding to the collection, rather than selling it off to pay for building repairs.

It was after four by the time he finally collapsed, famished, into a chair at his kitchen table. A plate of sandwiches that had been left on the table for him for whenever he finally wandered in sat in front of him. He realised he hadn't even stopped for lunch. Being a duke in the twenty-first century was much the same as being a CEO of a company. It was an exhausting role that needed every one of his skill sets and every ounce of his energy. It was then that his phone finally pinged.

@SohoJane: Hey there, sorry about the radio silence. I collapsed with exhaustion not long after your message. Are you back home?

He exhaled the breath he'd been holding for the past two days.

@FarmerDan: Yes, back home and back to the grind.

He pulled up one of the photos of the newborn lamb he'd taken that morning and sent it to her. She sent back half a dozen love hearts.

When it came to the farm he did what needed doing, but welcoming baby animals was one of his favourite parts.

CHAPTER TWO

LAURA SLOWED HER car as she rounded the corner and the castle came into view.

The structure was built over several eras: the front part of the building looked as though it had been built in the eighteenth century, made primarily from the distinctive Cotswold stone, a honey-coloured limestone that glowed golden in the sunlight. It looked more like a grand Georgian manor than a castle, but either way it was stunning.

The driveway led to a deserted car park and a small building, with a sign proclaiming *Abney Castle—Entry*. Beyond that was a brick wall stretching off into the distance in both directions. In front of her was a wrought-iron gate, shut and labelled with a closed sign.

They were expecting her, but it still felt inauspicious to be met with a locked gate. She noticed a box that appeared to be an intercom and wound down her window. She pressed the button and a camera swirled in her direction. After a while she heard the line open. 'Good afternoon, how may I help?'

'I'm Laura Oliver. From…' The gate clicked and slowly parted. The voice at the other end of the line was gone.

Laura drove her small car slowly along the drive, taking in the lush green lawns, the magnificent vista sloping up to the front of the castle. The gravel drive led her directly to the front door where she stopped her car, but didn't turn off the engine. What next? Did she just park here and then knock on the door? She looked at the front door, if you could call it that. Double sided, painted a deep red with a knocker that might or might not be real gold. It was as wide and high as a double-decker bus.

Before she could decide, a single door to the side of the double entrance opened and a middle-aged woman with a friendly smile and a quick step came out and over to Laura's car.

'Laura! Welcome to Abney Castle. If you wouldn't mind driving around to the side of the building, I'll show you to the cottage.'

Laura nodded and drove as instructed to the side of the hall and turned the corner. There again was a further stretch of gravel drive, which she drove along slowly, following the woman.

Laura had been in amazing buildings before; she'd met nobility before. She'd been behind the scenes of the Louvre, the National Gallery and the Rijksmuseum. But this felt different. She was being invited into someone's home.

She felt the full honour of this assignment, and silently thanked her former mentor, Archibald, for recommending she take on this work on his behalf. Being given the responsibility of looking after a collection as important as this would be a highlight of her career.

The crunch of the gravel was crisp under her tyres. Along the driveway flower beds overflowed with spring colour. The woman led her to a wisteria-covered thatched cottage, half hidden in the grove of birch trees. It looked like it had been ripped from the pages of a Cotswold tourist catalogue.

This was her cottage.

'Laura, I'm Claudia, the family housekeeper at Abney Castle and this is where you'll be staying. Come on, let me show you around.'

Claudia unlocked the wooden door to the cottage and then handed Laura the keys. 'Those keys also have the clicker to unlock the front gate, so you can feel free to come and go as you please. Of course, the village is actually a one-mile walk, that way.' She pointed in the opposite direction to the one Laura had come from. 'There is a key for that gate as well. Access is only by foot that way, but those are the two entrances you will most likely need.'

Claudia barely drew breath and Laura was still processing all the information, as well as her beautiful surroundings as Claudia led her into the cottage.

The ceiling was low, as to be expected in such a cottage. At least two or three hundred years old, maybe more, though it was fully renovated and modernised, while keeping the original charm.

'This is your sitting room.'

The room was furnished with two soft sofas covered in floral fabrics. There was a fireplace and a large television.

'Through there is the kitchen-diner. I've left some groceries in the fridge for you, but you'll need to do some shopping at some stage.'

'Thank you, you didn't have to.'

'Nonsense. Let me know if you want me to add anything to the order, but if you want to do your own, the village has a very good store. And down the back—' Claudia led the way down a narrow hall '—are the two bedrooms. They are both made up. I expect you would prefer the larger, but just in case the other is ready to go as well. And in case you want to have visitors.'

'I didn't…that is…' Flummoxed, it hadn't even occurred to Laura that she might be allowed to have guests.

'Of course, just let me know so I can tell security. And if you plan on having any wild parties—'

'I would never—'

'Then just make sure you invite me!' She laughed heartily and Laura wondered if she was joking or not. As if she'd throw a wild party in this gorgeous cottage. It didn't scream 'all-night raver'. Rather 'curl up with a book by the fire'.

'I will be sure to, but I expect I'll be too busy with the paintings to throw any wild parties.'

'Yes, about that. The duke is expected back later this afternoon. He'd like to show you the house and the paintings himself, if that's okay?'

The duke wanted to see her himself? She thought she'd be dealing with the estate manager or someone from the castle museum.

'Yes, of course.'

'So feel free to unpack, get yourself settled and even have an explore of the grounds. You're lucky to arrive on a Tuesday, when we're closed. The weekdays aren't too bad but on a weekend, the place swarms with day trippers. You'll have the whole place to yourself today. And the weather's splendid!'

After saying goodbye to Claudia, Laura collapsed into the nearest sofa and exhaled, her head spinning.

The duke would be here, showing her the castle personally. That was unexpected; as far as she could tell from the photographs online he was quite elderly, well into his eighties. Not that people that age couldn't be fit, but it did seem like unnecessary effort to go to show her around. He must be very proud of his collection. Or attached to it. She hoped she was equal to the task of looking after it.

After a phone call to her mother letting her know she'd arrived, Laura unpacked and explored the cottage.

Claudia had indeed stocked the pantry and the fridge. There was a plate of sandwiches and two home-cooked meals with handwritten labels and cooking instructions. Shepherd's pie and vegetable curry. She salivated but took out the sandwiches.

The pantry was also generously stocked, tea bags in a variety of flavours, coffee pods also and two bottles of wine, a red and white. Laura made herself a cup of tea, opening several cupboards until she located everything. She ate the sandwiches as she checked in at work and read her emails.

When she'd finished, it was still only just after one and she wondered if she had a few hours to spare before the duke arrived. She didn't want to miss him and wasn't sure what 'late afternoon' meant, exactly, but figured she had time to explore the grounds and maybe even walk to the village. She gathered her phone and the keys, debated whether she'd need a jacket, but given the blue sky and gentle breeze, decided against it. At the last minute she dug through her bag for a sticky note.

'Gone for a walk, back soon, Laura' she wrote followed by her phone number. She affixed it to the front door in case the duke arrived while she was out. She didn't want to inconvenience any boss, let alone an elderly duke.

She made her way down the side of the castle and once she reached the corner, the full expanse of the building and its grounds came into view. The back of Abney Castle was every bit as impressive as the front. Unlike the front facade, which was all Georgian elegance, the back of the building showed more hints of the older history of the castle with smaller windows and some medieval-style pointed arches and turrets. Three generous stories high plus attics—the castle was beautiful.

The garden was equally impressive. Immediately before her lay a formal terraced garden, carefully designed in the French style with low hedges, innumerable flowers, fountains and statues. Beyond that, and stretching out to the horizon were the famous gardens designed in the English landscape style to look natural, but truly every blade of grass and every stone was meant to be exactly where it was. A stream gurgled off into the distance, forded by a pretty stone bridge. Laura hardly knew where to begin, but the bridge called to her. She wanted to walk along it.

The air smelt of roses and freshly cut grass and the oxygen filled her lungs like a balm. The sky was the bright blue of a spring day and she had the entire place to herself. She gave a quiet chuckle. Life was funny, a few months ago she'd been at one of her lowest moments ever and now, here she was, temporarily at home in some of the most beautiful gardens in the country.

The path to the bridge took her past ponds filled with fish, ducks and geese. Once she reached the bridge she crossed it, stopped halfway and looked back up to the castle. She couldn't believe she was getting paid to be here.

The grounds must have an army of gardeners looking after it, the castle too. But for the moment at least it was simply hers to enjoy.

She heard the sound of a barking dog behind a hedge and went to investigate. She didn't want one of the gardeners finding her and thinking she had no business being there. She rounded the corner of the hedge and saw two golden cocker spaniels barking and dancing around one another. And something else she couldn't quite make out at first.

As she approached the scene came into focus. It was a man. And an animal of some sort. A calf. Or a small cow. Both the man and the cow were on the other side of the wire fence from Laura. He was struggling and then she saw the problem. The calf appeared to be tangled in the wire.

Each time the man pulled the wire away, the calf inserted its head into the hole. He would steady the calf, but then the wire would pull tighter. He needed three or four hands for the task, yet he only had the usual allocation of two.

He was tall, well-built, and she paused and watched him for a while admiring the way the muscles in his shoulders flexed and rippled as he wrestled the calf.

The man was dressed in blue jeans, which nicely fit his strong thighs and bottom. His T-shirt looked as though it had once been white but was now a kaleidoscope of stains, mud, sweat and something else she didn't want to contemplate. Despite the mud and sweat, or maybe because of it, she wondered if the gardener was single and whether a country fling might just be the exact thing she needed.

He's not a gardener, he's a farmer.

FarmerDan?

No. It couldn't be. Dan would have told her if he worked for a duke, wouldn't he? The man had dark blond hair, just like Dan had. Could it be?

She heard the man curse and was jolted out of her thoughts.

Laura approached him and said. 'Here, let me help.'

His head spun and he regarded her with a mix of confusion and surprise. 'Do you know what you're doing?' he asked.

'Not in the slightest, but it looks like you don't either.'

Up close he was even more handsome; never mind his shoulders and thighs, the man had piercing blue eyes, framed by a strong brow and defined cheekbones. Resolutely handsome. If he looked good this filthy she really wanted to see how he'd look washed and clean.

No. This wasn't the time or the place.

'It does look like you could do with another set of hands,' she offered.

He sighed the sigh of a man who didn't want to accept help but knew he had no choice.

'I can't promise your clothes won't end up as another casualty.'

'I'm not precious and they wash.'

'If you're sure.'

She nodded.

'Then, if you step over here and hold up that part of the fence.'

She did as she was told, but pulling on one part of the wire only seemed to pull another tighter. The man had a hold of the calf with both hands now.

'And maybe, if you can reach, just there, above its ear.'

Laura stretched her arm, suddenly conscious that she was now very close to the man. Close enough that if she'd leant down just a little she could have pressed her lips to the back of his neck. It was a strong neck; veins protruded through the tan skin from the exertion and Laura's mouth went dry.

She wasn't really contemplating a fling with a gardener, was she? Or was she simply overcome by all the fresh country air?

The calf squealed and with a final grunt the man pulled the calf free.

It stood back, shook itself and then bolted away. The man stepped back, caught his breath and wiped his hands on his jeans. It did no good. His jeans were just as filthy as his hands.

Once he recovered his breath, he looked her up and down. Not in an appraising manner, just in an apparent effort to figure out who she was.

'Hello. May I ask who you are and what you're doing here?'

'I'm Laura Oliver. I've come to help the duke with the art collection. I was told I could have a look around the gardens while I waited for him to return. And you?'

His jaw dropped, and he nodded, his head bobbing up and down for too many beats, like he was putting some puzzle pieces together.

'Laura, welcome to Abney Castle. I'd offer you my hand but I wouldn't recommend you take it.'

'Thank you?'

She could see him gathering his composure before saying, 'I'm the Duke of Brighton.'

No. The Duke of Brighton was eighty if he were a day.

'But you're...' Handsome? Hot? Strong? 'Younger than I was expecting.'

He coughed. 'Thank you?'

She realised her faux pas the second before he said, 'You may be thinking of my father.'

Suddenly she wished she were the one covered in animal excrement; it would've been less embarrassing than this. 'I'm so, so sorry, Your Grace. I saw the photo on the website and assumed...'

'It's fine, really. We really should get that thing updated. He did pass away nearly a year ago now.'

'I'm so sorry for your loss. My father passed away nearly ten years ago, but I remember at one year, it was still raw.'

She couldn't meet his eye. *Ground, swallow me up.* Her embarrassment was mixed with disappointment; he wasn't Dan. Of course he wasn't. And she was far too obsessed with Dan for her own good. She was meant to be having a break from dating until she figured out what she was going to do with her body.

She heard him say softly, 'Laura, it really is okay. Thank you again for your help with the calf.' His voice was kind and the last trace of frustration and awkwardness seem to melt away from him.

She looked up and met his eyes. They lifted slightly at the edges into a soft smile. Friendly. Familiar. And yet how could they be?

The Duke of Brighton. The owner of Abney Castle, was standing across a broken wire fence from her, dripping in sweat and goodness knew what else. Like a smellier, dirtier, version of Colin Firth after his dip in the lake.

Were modern-day dukes allowed to be this hot? Weren't they all old, stuffy and not at all capable of untangling a precocious calf from a fence?

Apparently not.

'I met Claudia. She said I was welcome to have a look around and that you would like to show me the inside of the house. I mean castle.'

He laughed, but she wasn't sure at what.

'We do just call it a house. And you should call me Henry.'

'Henry,' she said, in confirmation. It was far easier than saying 'Your Grace'.

'I apologise again, I didn't realise I'd be dealing directly with you.'

'That's all right. I was particularly interested to meet you.'

He was? How odd.

'Claudia's our housekeeper. She looks after my mother and me and our apartments, but also the cottage and your needs. If you need anything, please feel free to start with her. But the main house is managed by a different team in entirely. That's overseen by Louis, who manages the guides, the cleaning. You'll meet him tomorrow. And the chief groundskeeper is Harvey, who is also away today. Tuesday is usually everyone's weekend. Hence, this falls to me.'

He pointed to the hole in the fence. 'As does giving you a tour of the house, but I hope that's more pleasant than this.'

He gestured to himself. 'If you could excuse me for a while, I think it's in everyone's interests if I shower before we do that.'

'Of course.'

He smiled at her and it was impossible not to smile back.

As if they knew it was their turn, the two dogs, golden spaniels who had been sitting patiently until now, began to bark again.

'And this pair are Buns and Honey.'

Laura laughed. 'Or Honey and Buns?'

'My mother named them. She thinks she's hilarious.'

'It's the kind of thing my mother would do too. May I pet them?'

He nodded. She loved dogs and this pair were beautiful.

'Good to meet you, Honey and Buns.'

At the sound of their names they stood and ran to her, putting their paws on the fence as if to reach for her.

She leant over the fence to pat them. She patted Buns, the boy, but Honey pushed her way in front so she settled for one hand on each, rubbing them behind their ears.

'You've made some friends. Do you have dogs?'

She shook her head. 'It's not practical in my apartment. But I do love them.'

'Once they know where you're staying they won't stay away.'

She couldn't help but smile. 'They're welcome anytime.'

She looked up and smiled, meeting the duke's gaze just as he was doing the same and his smile hit her with a force that almost made her breathless.

Uh-oh.

Wasn't her life complicated enough? She didn't need to add *Get a stomach-flipping crush on a duke* to the list.

CHAPTER THREE

IT WAS HER. The feeling in his chest told him it was her, yet she had a different name.

You didn't use your real name either.

Could the conservator sent by the museum be *his* SohoJane?

No. That would too much of a coincidence.

And yet, how many art conservators who specialised in nineteenth-century British oil paintings were there?

Probably more than you realise.

She'd told him she had had a big career opportunity. Was coming to Abney Castle what she'd meant?

When Laura had walked away, Henry took out his phone and brought up the profile picture he'd studied many times in order to get a better idea of what Jane looked like. Her profile photo wasn't entirely clear. She had her back to the sun, her face mostly obscured in the shade. A second photo was sharper, but she stood at a great distance. When he zoomed in on her face all he saw were blurry pixels. He knew. He'd tried hundreds of times. But this woman, Laura, did look like the two photos he'd seen of SohoJane.

She wanted anonymity on the dating site and he could hardly complain because he did too.

He'd also used a real photo of him—he wasn't about to steal someone's identity—but his face too was half hidden in the shadows. He didn't want someone doing a reverse image search and discovering who he really was. Not until he was ready to tell them.

Could it really be her? He wasn't sure, but he didn't have a clue how to subtly find out.

After temporarily securing the fence with some pliers and some spare wire he had on the truck, he drove back to the house. He got out of his soiled clothes and had a shower that was as hot as he could bear. It was hardly the first time he'd found himself covered in mud and animal fluids but the first time he'd been caught like that by a beautiful woman.

A woman he wanted to make a good impression in front of.

That realisation made something shift uneasily inside him.

If she wasn't SohoJane, then what would it mean if he liked Laura too?

Nothing, because you aren't currently dating either of them.

Henry was a pure monogamist; he didn't have feelings for two women at one time, let alone relationships, but his attraction to Laura sat uncomfortably with him, even though what he had with Jane was purely platonic.

And Laura worked for him.

So he really shouldn't be thinking about *either* of them in that way.

You could just ask her if she's SohoJane?

He laughed aloud at the thought. He wasn't about to come right out and say, *Hey, are you SohoJane on the A Deux dating site?*

He shook his head. No. But he had to say something, didn't he?

He stood for a long while in front of his open closet, a walk-in arrangement that was full of clean, pressed outfits, suitable for a duke. And not one of them felt appropriate for this meeting. His father would have worn a suit and tie, but that was too much for Henry. Jeans and T-shirt felt too much like work wear. He settled on some brown trousers and a dark blue fitted shirt and studied himself in the mirror. Normally he didn't think twice about his outfits; his tailor always ensured his clothes fit perfectly and theoretically anything in this wardrobe should be suitable.

But what if Laura *was* SohoJane?

Should he have said something when he first

saw her? If he'd had his wits about him, their first conversation might have played out differently.

'I'm the Duke of Brighton. But please call me Henry. Daniel is a family name, my middle name and the name I use in my dating profile. Ring any bells? And you look familiar, you aren't SohoJane by any chance?'

Of course he hadn't said that. Apart from anything else he'd been covered in cow manure, surprised by her presence and nearly knocked breathless by the sight of the beautiful woman in front of him. At the first sight of her blue eyes it had been a wonder he'd been able to say anything at all.

After changing the blue shirt for a green one, he made his way out of his apartments and across to the cottage.

Both Henry and his mother, the duchess, or dowager duchess as she officially was, had private apartments at one end of the castle. They were smaller and less extravagant than the main rooms that were open to the public. Yet they had undergone modern renovations and were far easier to heat, cool and maintain. His mother spent most of her time at their London residence, Brighton House in Mayfair, but she came and went from Abney with a pattern he'd never been able to ascertain. As long as she was still driving and independent he figured things were well with her and he had no need to worry. She'd spoken of moving out of Brighton House and into her own place several times since Henry's father passed away, but Henry assured her there was no need. When he did marry, they might all reassess Caroline's living arrangements, but until then he was happy to share the castle and the London house with her. With over two hundred rooms between the two residences, they were hardly in one another's pockets.

Laura was waiting outside the cottage. As she walked towards him, excitement rose up inside him, but he pushed it quickly down. Laura was here in a professional capacity, for all intents and purposes as his employee. His family had an enduring relationship with the firm for which she worked and he couldn't ruin that.

He smiled, clasped his hands behind his back and tried to ignore how sweaty they had suddenly become as he watched her approach him across the lawn. She had changed out of her jeans into a long woollen green dress, and high black boots. Her dark hair was loose and flowed in silken waves around her shoulders.

She was beautiful.

He ignored that thought too.

Even if she is SohoJane, nothing can happen

*between you. She's taking a break from dating.
She's been clear about that from the beginning.*

'Your Grace.' Laura greeted him with an outstretched hand.

'Henry, I told you.'

'I know, I'm trying to pretend, for your sake as much as mine, that our first meeting didn't happen.'

He suppressed a smile. In this new outfit she looked professional and stylish.

And edible.

He was in trouble.

'Did you get very soiled? Please send your clothes up to the house and we can wash them properly for you. Sadly, we're not strangers to that sort of mess.'

She waved the suggestion away. 'I missed it all.'

'Yes, well.' The sooner they changed the subject from cow manure the better. 'Shall we?' He motioned to the house.

'Yes please. Can I just say first of all that it's an absolute honour to be here. Archibald was my mentor, he was a great conservator.'

'The honour's ours. And I'm sorry to hear that he passed away. Did you know he personally recommended you take over from him?'

She nodded, but looked sombre.

'Yes, as a matter of fact he'd written it in the file. It was…'

She had this habit of tucking her long hair behind her ears when she was nervous. Or affected. She did it now. 'I was very touched to read it. I miss him a lot.'

Henry had met the man a few times over the years. 'He was a character.'

'Indeed, but amazing at his job. Which is good for you. His notes of your collection are meticulous and go back decades.'

Henry nodded. He supposed this was a good thing but honestly did not have a great idea what art conservation actually entailed. Being a duke involved wearing a lot of hats, many of which he was only just learning.

'I'm so sorry again about not knowing about your father. I should've done more research.'

'It's all right, truly. We really should update the castle's website.'

Since his father died, he had, subconsciously, or otherwise, avoided any announcements or publicity that were not strictly necessary. It suited him for the wider world to not realise he was now the duke. It suited him that everyone else thought of his father as the duke. For crying out loud, most days, he struggled to think of himself as the duke.

You should tell her now. That you're Farmer-Dan.

No. He needed to make sure it was really her first. He had a strong suspicion, but there was no certainty that the gorgeous woman next to him now was the same woman he'd been chatting to for months.

Besides, SohoJane had made it clear, she didn't want to meet. Not him, not anyone. She had something personal going on was all she'd said and he hadn't pressed. Despite telling him she was stepping away from dating, she'd kept talking to him. That was a sign of their friendship and her trust in him. He couldn't come out now and spring this on her. Could he?

He'd wait to say anything. Apologise later, if necessary.

'Why is it called a castle? If you don't mind me saying, it looks more like a house. I mean, not that it's not amazing,' she said as he opened one of the front doors.

'I'll get to that part of the tour.'

'I can't wait.'

There was a twinkle in her eye that lit up the blue with a golden spark. Inside his chest hitched and his mouth went dry. Again.

It wasn't as though he wasn't meant to be dating: he was. He was the duke now; there was no heir, let alone a spare. He had to, as they said, get cracking and find a wife. It shouldn't have been an unpleasant task, or even a painful one. But somehow it was.

He'd been burnt too many times before. Women

saw the title. They saw the castle and rarely looked past those two things to see him. Really see him. That was one reason why SohoJane was so special. That was why he was persevering with the A Deux app to begin with.

Laura was attractive, and so far she seemed lovely. Trustworthy.

Though she was saying all the usual things women said about the castle—*It's beautiful, it's amazing...*

Do you want her to tell you that it's ugly?

Not at all. She was a conservator so actually knew about art and probably also architecture and history. She wasn't gushing because she had a tiara in her sights, but because she had a genuine interest.

Ever since Beatrice he'd never quite been able to trust anyone who was overly fascinated with Abney Castle. Beatrice had been his girlfriend at university, the first woman he'd ever loved. He'd thought they'd marry, he thought he was so lucky to have found the love of his life so young, so easily. He'd been mistaken all along.

'Would you like the quick tour or the long one?'

'Do you have anywhere to be?'

'I have a date with BBC One and the French Open at eight p.m., but apart from that, no.'

She laughed, but if she was SohoJane then she

might piece it together? SohoJane knew about his love of tennis.

'I'll show you everywhere you need to know about, but you should still feel free to explore yourself. Please go wherever you need to. The family apartments have a separate entrance so you won't stumble in on me by accident.'

'And the rest of your family?'

Did he imagine the quaver in her voice when she asked this or was it wishful thinking? 'It's just me and my mother and she spends most of her time in London.'

'So, it's just you living here?' Her voice rose at the end of the sentence.

'Yes, Claudia and Louis both live in houses on that side of the castle.' He motioned in the direction from which Laura had entered the grounds. 'And a few other staff live in the village, but generally it's just me in the house.'

She raised an eyebrow, but he couldn't interpret the look. Was it judgement? Or something else entirely?

She didn't say anything more.

Henry saw the treasures of Abney Castle with fresh eyes as he led Laura around. She would be examining the contents of most rooms in detail over the course of her visit. He simply wanted her to become acquainted with the house and show her the layout. Maybe the secret, private passages.

He delighted in her gasps and sighs at each new room, bursting with pride as if he'd built the place himself. Which was silly. He was going to have to check his emotions where Laura was concerned.

He showed her into one of the main bedrooms. Last slept in by his great-grandfather but decorated by his mother in a mid-Victorian style. The ornate four-poster bed was nearly as tall as the high ceiling and was covered in opulent velvet drapes that fell all the way to the intricate Persian carpet on the floor.

'Did you grow up here?' she asked, spying the bed. He didn't think it looked particularly comfortable and as a rule they avoided sitting on the old furniture, but suddenly the image of Laura sitting on the edge of the bed and beckoning him over to her popped into his head.

He was the duke. It was his furniture. He could do what he wanted with it…

But that was not a helpful thought.

'Partly. But not in these rooms. My grandfather's generation was the last to live in this part of the house. When he married my grandmother they adapted the apartments for the family to live in and began to restore and preserve these rooms.'

'Did it take a long time? It looks to be in good condition.'

'Thank you, and yes. It was a lifetime project for both of them. They started just after the Second World War and began opening up rooms to the public in the nineteen sixties.'

'They did an amazing job,' she said spinning slowly in the room. 'But it still must be a lot of work to maintain. Let alone clean.'

He smiled to himself. Beatrice had asked questions such as how much it had cost. Laura, clearly a conservator, was only interested in the cleaning.

'It is. But I have a great team who work with me and who love the castle as much as I do.'

Being a twenty-first-century duke wasn't about being waited upon, it was about mucking in with everyone else to clean, manage. And get calves unstuck from fences.

But it was a privilege. And his duty. He meant to see the estate, including the castle, passed on down just as it had been passed down to him. After all the hard work and good management of his forefathers, he didn't want to be the one to see the castle, or the estates, fall into ruin.

After taking her through all the rooms that were open to the public he took her to a door marked *Private—No Entry*.

'Now you've had the public tour, let me take you out the back.'

She smiled and his heart hit his throat. Regardless of who she was, he was going to have to learn to tame the physical reactions he was having around her.

The corridors and rooms behind the scenes were simply painted in whites and greys and mostly unfurnished. It was difficult enough keeping the main rooms in order—it was only family and staff that saw these rooms. They were mostly offices and storage rooms and corridors that connected the other rooms with passages that had once been used by the servants.

'Importantly, this is the staff room.' He pointed into a large room, furnished in a mismatch of periods but with a small kitchen and a large television.

Henry led her down the corridor and into the next room. 'This room was where Archibald set himself up. Hopefully there's enough room for you to work in here.'

'This is great.' She looked around the large, light-filled workshop, equipped with some easels, tables, chairs and another kitchenette. 'What was this room originally?'

'I've no idea. It was Archibald's for as long as I can remember. He insisted he needed it to be north facing.'

'That's right, we try to work as much as possible with the best light available.'

'If you need anything else, just let me or Louis

know and we will take care of it. And if you need
to move any of the larger paintings…'

'Ask first?'

'No, I trust you. I was going to say, ask someone to help you lift them.'

'Thank you.'

When she smiled at him, grateful, eyes spar-
kling, he wanted to spin her into his arms. Could
he date Laura? She worked for him, but that didn't
have to be an insurmountable barrier. He liked
her; it would be foolish to deny it. But could she
like him? Would she see past the title to the man
behind it?

It was a question that was impossible to answer
at the moment, seeing how he was currently en-
gaged with showing her around his castle. And
for the first time in years he wanted to show it off.

'Would you like to see why it's called a castle?'

'Yes please.'

He led the way down the nearest staircase and
out a side door. At this side of the building the
land sloped away sharply, down to the river. Unlike on the other side of the building, this land
was now mostly wild, not cultivated or curated
garden, but it still afforded a sweeping view of
the valley below. 'There's been a fortification on
this hill since Norman times. Some stones from
the original keep still remain, but this part of the
castle was built in the fourteenth century.'

Henry took out his keys and unlocked the gate that now blocked their path. It squeaked when he pushed it open. Laura entered first and pride welled up inside him. He could tell she saw it as he did, with appreciation of the history and a desire to look after it. Not with pound signs in her eyes.

What Beatrice, what many other women he met, didn't understand was that he didn't see the castle as his. It was his family's. His children's. He held it all in trust for the future. Far from being able to relax and enjoy his property, it was his job to maintain it.

Even though Henry wanted to find a woman he could trust would love him—Henry Daniel Weston—even he had a hard time separating himself from his title. It was the reason for his very existence, his very birth. Was he being foolish wanting someone to see him in a way he hardly did himself?

He felt Laura's soft sigh in his chest when the trees parted and the structure came into view. 'This was a working castle for over three hundred years. During the Wars of the Roses and Tudor times. Queen Elizabeth I even visited on one of her progresses. But this was the structure that suffered a direct hit during the Civil War and rather than repair it, they built the house next to it, but the name Abney Castle stuck.'

'Is it open to the public?' Laura asked as they made their way around the ivy-covered ruins. The footprint of the fourteenth-century structure was mostly visible, though the roof had long gone and a few of the walls were missing. He took her to his favourite part, an intact wall where the Gothic-shaped window frames were still intact.

'It's not safe—for the public or the structure. We want to preserve it, but it's difficult. Some preservation attempts last century did more damage than good.'

'Yes, it's a trade-off I understand well. The first rule of conservation is do no harm.'

'Like Hippocrates?"

She laughed. 'I guess so.'

'It was open, a few years ago now, but we've closed it until we can get a proper survey done. Preserving medieval ruins is not a cheap business. Nor a common one.'

'I don't suppose it is.'

She knew all this stuff—why was he telling her all of this? As an art conservator she probably knew more about this than he did, but he couldn't seem to be able to stop talking.

'My father thought about handing it over to the National Trust. They may be able to do more than we can.'

'But he didn't?'

'No. They had some discussions, but my father

decided that keeping the estate all together and in the family was the better option. He hoped to be able to raise enough money to come up with his own conservation plan.'

Laura brushed past him and he smelt roses. His stomach flipped.

'It's amazing,' she said. 'I can't believe this was in your backyard growing up.'

'It is something else.' And something to live up to.

'So much history. Your ancestors lived here. Your great-great-great…never mind. It would take too long.'

'There have been Westons here since the twelfth century, though Thomas Weston wasn't made duke until the reign of James the First.'

'I'm not even sure who my great-great-grand-parents were. It's amazing that you know so much about your family.'

'It's a privilege.'

It wasn't just the title that he had to be proud of, it was this entire place. Even the moss-covered stones beneath his feet.

'It's been here for nine hundred years and hope-fully another nine hundred. I'm just the caretaker.'

She scoffed. 'I think you're a little more than that.'

'Not really. It's my job to look after this whole

place and leave it in a better condition than I found it.'

She gave him that look again, a flicker of her eyebrows. Doubting. Or surprise. He didn't know her well enough yet to be able to tell. All he knew was that when she looked into his eyes everything else in the world faded out.

'It was my father's philosophy, and my grandparents' as well. I intend to pass all of this onto my son. Or daughter.'

She coughed. 'We should get back. I've taken up enough of your time.'

As they walked back he asked, 'Do you have everything you need?'

'Yes, my equipment is all in my car. But if you have a spare ladder...'

'I'll see that you get one. But ask Louis tomorrow if you have any trouble.'

When they reached the front door to her cottage he wished, for the first time in his life, that the castle was bigger so that they could keep talking. Laura stopped and shifted her weight from one foot to the other. 'Thank you again.'

'It was a pleasure. I truly hope you don't get lost.'

She smiled and the sensation he felt in his chest when she did was starting to feel familiar. He smiled back and contemplated asking her out for a drink or dinner but her expression suddenly changed.

'First off, I will assess the paintings, check for damage, prepare a condition report on what needs to be done. You will look that over and then, depending on what needs doing, I can start work.' Her tone was businesslike.

He nodded.

'It's impossible to say how long it will take, but I understand that Archibald usually spent a few weeks or a month here. Is that okay?'

'Anything and everything you need. And don't feel like you need to rush. You're welcome to stay as long as you like.'

'I may need to go home for a week or so in the middle of my stay.'

The firm had said it could be a possibility that Laura would need to break up her visit but hadn't said anything more than that it was 'due to personal circumstances.'

'If we can play things by ear, that would be great.'

'Yes. The guides know you'll be working here. You can ask Louis for anything. Claudia as well. And me. I will be around tomorrow.' He took a business card from his pocket and handed it to her. 'Please call if there's anything you need, but go wherever you want to. The entire castle is at your disposal.'

'Thank you. I will. And I'll let you get on with your evening. I really appreciate you taking the time to give me a tour.'

She waved goodbye and left him standing at her front door like an fool, regretting he hadn't just asked her out for a drink to welcome her to the area.

Regretting he hadn't figured out a way to find out if she really was SohoJane.

He walked back into the castle to check everything was locked up properly. The rooms and corridors were now dimly lit, the sun close to setting. He liked some rooms here more than others; each held memories—and not only his, but he could feel those of his ancestors in many of them. Most of all he could feel his father. Sometimes he even fancied he could feel his brother. His older brother, Daniel, who had died before Henry was born. Daniel who would have been the thirteenth duke if he hadn't fallen under his horse.

Daniel was a strange shadowy presence in Henry's life. When he was little he was kind of like an imaginary friend, and Henry didn't quite understand that they would never actually meet.

But as Henry got older, when he turned eighteen, he realised he was now the older brother. That he was older than Daniel ever would be. That he would go to university, travel…do things that Daniel would never do.

Including becoming a duke.

That was why he had been born in the first place. It was literally his reason for existing.

Henry sat on one of the visitor chairs in the great hall and took out his phone.

@FarmerDan: Hi there, how was your day?

@SohoJane: Wonderful!

Could this be her? The tour of the house might be described as 'wonderful' but the run-in with the cow?

@FarmerDan: I'm all ears.

@SohoJane: Work was great, my new assignment feels a bit like a fairytale.

@FarmerDan: With a handsome prince?

Or a handsome duke?

@SohoJane: Ha-ha. How was your day?

He looked at his phone and planned his next response carefully.

@FarmerDan: It was pretty good, apart from a run-in with a feisty cow.

He couldn't concentrate on anything while he waited for her response.

@SohoJane: You mean the four-legged type, right?

@FarmerDan: Of course!!!

@SohoJane: Ouch, sounds painful. Are you okay?

@FarmerDan: Fine, the only bruise was to my ego.

It didn't seem that she recognised the situation. If she did, wouldn't she have said, 'What a coincidence, me too'?

It wasn't her.

Laura wasn't SohoJane.

So where did that leave him? Attracted to two women at once? That felt all wrong.

Jane doesn't want to date you. Or anyone.

He should get to know Laura better. She was bright, gorgeous. Good company. They seemed to have a lot in common. She certainly seemed to fall into the 'eligible' category.

But he didn't want just anyone.

He wanted *Jane*.

He wouldn't be able to date anyone else seriously until he'd met her or knew what her secret was. What was keeping her from meeting him. What was keeping her from dating.

@FarmerDan: No pressure, but maybe the next time I'm in London we could have a drink. As friends. I know you're not looking for anything else.

@SohoJane: You're incorrigible.

Henry groaned. He'd gone too far. But a second later another message flashed up on his screen.

@SohoJane: But I'll think about it.

This was closer than she'd ever come before. Maybe it would happen soon.

But what if his feelings for Laura continued to grow in the meantime?

He looked up at the painting of the third Duke of Brighton staring down smugly at him. As well he might. 'You don't know how lucky you were, never having to date online,' Henry said to the painting.

CHAPTER FOUR

BACK INSIDE THE COTTAGE, Laura's head spun. As Laura suspected, Henry looked only more handsome when he was showered and changed. He smelt good too. She'd caught faint traces of an understated aftershave when he'd held a door open for her or brushed past her. *He probably feels good as well*, she thought with a sigh.

He wasn't married. He lived alone.

What would it be like to be a duchess? She shook the thought away even before it was fully formed. It was his duty to have heirs. That fact alone would exclude her from the duchess contest. But another, more pressing, more urgent idea crept in. What would it be like to sleep with Henry?

She laughed. Probably great.

Probably so great there must be a queue of women waiting to bed him.

If Abney Castle wasn't a big enough turn-on, then surely Henry himself with his strong arms and tight glutes would be enough to make the women—or the men—line up.

Just as well. She wasn't interested in Henry. He was as good as her employer. And then there was Dan.

At the thought of him, her phone buzzed with a message.

@FarmerDan: Hi, there, how was your day?

Laura messaged him back, telling him as much as she could about her day without giving away anything about where she was. And it sounded like Dan had had an eventful day with a cow as well. What was it with the Cotswolds and cows?

And FarmerDan likes tennis.

And he lives in Gloucestershire...

No! That was ridiculous. Dan wasn't a duke. He was *Dan*.

Her thoughts leapt back to the first moment she'd seen him wrestling the cow, how she'd wondered if that farmer could be *her* farmer.

She immediately pulled up his profile photo.

Dan looked blond, at least with the sun behind him. And his hair was longer. And Dan was a farmer! Not a duke. And he had a different name. She could believe that a duke might want a degree of anonymity but why not just go with Farmer-Henry?

No. It couldn't be him.

Lots of people had cows in Gloucestershire. Lots of people were following the French Open.

She squinted and zoomed in so far the image became unclear, but she still couldn't be sure.

Could she ask him?

No, she couldn't. Besides, it wasn't him. Dukes didn't need dating apps. They had an entire society of aristocrats trying to set them up with eligible misses.

Laura took off her boots, turned on the oven and put in the pie Claudia had kindly made her. Then she poured herself a glass of the white wine.

But if Henry was single…and she was here for a while. She shook the thought away as well. She already had enough on her plate. With the job. Her health. And Dan.

Besides, she wasn't the type to be interested in two men at once. It made her uncomfortable. Not to mention exhausted.

She wasn't ready for one relationship at the moment, let alone two.

Laura woke five minutes before her alarm, fully rested and alert. The country air must agree with her. Either that or the fact that she had a magic key to a castle!

'Go wherever you need. The entire castle is at your disposal.'

She dressed professionally but practically in

navy pants and a white shirt, and tied her long hair back away from her face. Today would likely involve a lot of walking and probably some heavy lifting as well. Thankfully, the small kitchen was equipped with a good coffee machine; Claudia was not one to skip an important detail like that.

Laura approached the castle and took in its loveliness, the famous Cotswold stone almost glowing in the morning light. She walked to the small entrance, the one Claudia had used and the one for which she had a key, but even as she turned it in the lock she half expected it not to turn. But it did, and with a satisfying click the door fell open.

The place was silent to begin with, but in less than an hour the first museum staff arrived and by midmorning a steady stream of visitors was wandering through the beautiful rooms.

Laura started out by assessing the size of the task and figuring out where everything was. Archibald had kept meticulous records of the collection over his years of involvement, which Laura had on her laptop. But despite his care, oil paintings needed to be regularly assessed. They could become acidic and brittle over time, leading to cracks developing. The timber frames could also degrade and distort, potentially damaging the canvas.

Her job was to check each item, consider whether it had deteriorated in the intervening years, and if and how it needed any cleaning or repair. Additionally, she had to check the position and manner in which each artwork was displayed or stored and recommend any environmental changes to help preserve the works.

There were over a hundred pieces on her initial review list. It was a big task, but the special surroundings meant it would be a pleasure.

The day passed so quickly Laura was surprised to notice that the visitors had disappeared and Louis was wishing her a good evening. She planned to work into the evening, but the sound of someone clearing their throat made her look up from her work on a Dante Gabriel Rossetti.

'Good day?'

It was Henry, but he was blurry, and she had to remove her magnifying glasses to see him properly.

She brushed herself off, despite not being covered in anything except a day's worth of hard work.

'Hey. How are you?'

He smiled broadly and she pushed her attraction down. She'd hoped that the belly flips of yesterday had been a blip, just caused by the whirlwind of being shown around a castle. But no. Her attraction to Henry was more than just that. It was physical and visceral and grabbed her right in the gut. He was wearing blue jeans, like yesterday, only clean, with a white shirt, loose with the top few buttons undone, giving her a tempting view of the tanned skin on his neck. Delicious. She had to swallow.

'What's the damage on this one?' he asked, leaning in and looking over her shoulder. Making her heart rate hitch up a few notches and her head light.

'It's not too bad, actually, but I'll have to clean it a little first to make sure. It is a truly beautiful collection. I mean, I'm familiar with most of the works but to see them in person—it's very special.'

Henry smiled shyly. 'I wish I could take credit for it, but alas, my ancestors were the ones with the foresight. I'm always looking at ways to expand the collection, even with more modern works. I am conscious of passing down a collection better than the one I've inherited.'

'I can give you a little advice on that, but I can also put you in touch with people who know a lot more about that than I do.'

She was trying to keep their conversation professional, that way she wouldn't notice how the temperature in the room seemed to have increased a few degrees since Henry entered. Why had he come by? Just to check up on her or…?

He looks edible.

Her stomach growled loudly at the thought and her face burnt.

Henry grinned. 'Please don't feel you have to say yes, but I was wondering if you'd like to join me for a meal in the village? The pub's great and I can show you the shortcut through the garden.'

Even though a part of her thought that spending time with Henry was probably not great for her peace of mind, this was exactly how she wanted to spend her evening.

'What about Roland-Garros?' she asked, remembering he liked tennis.

'It'll wait.'

'Okay, that'd be great. Thanks.'

One hour later, fresh out of the shower, Laura looked at the contents of her suitcase. It was the second day in a row she was dressing for a date with a duke. Not that this was a date, date. It was an appointment, but she'd packed mostly plain working clothes and hadn't anticipated wanting to dress a little bit special. It had been months since she'd felt the need—or the desire—to dress up.

It's a country pub! Your jeans will be fine!

She slipped on her jeans and a white T-shirt and grabbed her blazer and scarf. The warm spring day was rapidly cooling to a fresh evening.

The sun was low in the sky as Henry led the way across the formal part of the garden, with its carefully designed garden beds planted with delphiniums and gardenias, to the less structured fields beyond.

She spotted the folly on a nearby hill. A stone building that looked like a small Hellenic temple. 'That's beautiful,' she remarked.

'Remind me to take you up there one day. It's not open to the public.'

'Why not?' It didn't seem as old or fragile as the castle ruins he had shown her yesterday.

'We have to maintain some mystery.' He winked at her and heat bloomed in her chest. Was he flirting with her? Surely not.

Why not? Why wouldn't he flirt with you? Laura, you've just been out of the game for so long. Men do find you attractive.

Once again, she was torn. She liked Henry, could almost contemplate a no strings attached fling. But she worked for him. And she wasn't meant to be getting entangled in anything at the moment. Even a fling.

He chatted to her as they walked along, pointing out things of interest, telling a few anecdotes about the place and before she knew it they had reached a high brick wall. She didn't notice it until they were upon it, as it was camouflaged by trees and shrubs.

'Wow.'

'I know. It's the way the ground dips here, it

gives the impression that the estate goes on for miles longer than it actually does.'

He unlocked a door in the middle of the wall and beyond it was a path leading to what she now saw was the nearby village of Abneyford. Like many Cotswold villages, Abneyford was picturesque.

'In summer this place is crawling with tourists, but tonight, it'll be mostly us locals.'

Henry led the way to a bustling pub, clearly the centre of the village. He was greeted by the barman and introduced her right away. 'Laura, this is Robert. He and his wife run the best pub in the county. Laura's our guest for the next few weeks, so look after her.'

'Of course we will.' Robert's smile was friendly. 'Are you after dinner?'

'Yes please.'

Henry took her through the menu at the bar like someone who had tried each dish multiple times. 'But the salmon is something to behold.'

'I'll have that then.'

They found a table for two in a quiet corner of the dining room. It was a typical traditional pub, with a low ceiling supported by dark beams, heavy furniture and years of laughter echoing in the walls.

'This place is probably as old as the castle,' Laura said.

'I'm not sure, but I can tell you the Weston family has been frequenting the pub since it opened.'

'Really? I would have thought they would have been waited on by all their servants.'

'The dukes had to meet their duchesses somewhere.'

She laughed. The thought was pretty preposterous. 'Surely your ancestors would have found their wives in London, at the marriage markets of the ton.'

'You'd be surprised. The eighth duke met his wife in the village when they were children and the tenth, my great-grandfather, married the head gardener's daughter.'

'Really?'

'Really. We have a proud tradition of not marrying the women expected of us.'

Again, was he flirting with her?

And how did she feel about it if he was?

Maybe it was the wine, maybe it was being away from home, but Laura couldn't help but flirt back.

'And what about you? Have you dated any of the barmaids? Have your eye on a local governess?'

He laid his arms on the table and leant forward. His blue eyes darkened as he said, 'I haven't married—or even dated—any governesses or barmaids.'

'I meant…' Her face was flushed. What did she mean? The walls were closing in on the two of them and she was having trouble keeping her heart rate steady and her thoughts in check.

'I do have to marry though,' he said.

'I'd expect so.'

'If I don't have a legitimate heir, the title dies with me.'

'It dies?'

'Yes. My father didn't have any siblings. I don't have any siblings.'

'There are no cousins?' Surely he could find a long-lost cousin somewhere willing to move into a castle.

'Some distant, but the letters patent establishing the dukedom mean it must be a direct heir of the current duke or one immediately preceding. It can pass to a male or a female, so they at least allow that.'

A wave of disappointment rolled over her, which was so ridiculous. She already knew he planned to have children—he'd told her that the day before. She and Henry could never have anything more than a flirtation. She knew this— whether he was a duke or not. There was a good chance she'd be having a hysterectomy in the next year or so; this was why she wasn't getting herself into situations like this where she was so attracted to a man she struggled to think straight. *This* was precisely why she'd stepped away from dating.

Thankfully, someone was smiling down on her because at that point Robert delivered their fish to the table and Laura didn't have to respond to what Henry had just said.

The food was as good as Henry had promised, and the wine happily warmed her insides. Henry was leaning across from her, asking her about her career and her life in London, and listening carefully hanging on every answer.

'Where did you grow up?'

'London, born and bred.'

'Where abouts?'

'I lived out in Kew when I was younger, but now I'm in Soho.' She had a shoebox-sized flat but loved how central she was to everything. 'It's certainly a lot busier than it is here.'

'I suppose you find all this deadly dull?' He gestured around the pub.

'Not at all, I'm having a great time. I love the city, but this is great as well.'

He asked her all about her job, hanging on her answers, though Laura didn't read much into that, she was there to look after his paintings after all. He asked her what made her decide to become a conservator and she told him the story about how, when she was fifteen and her grandmother had died, Laura had been shocked to find out that there were no photos of her beloved grand-mother as a child. Some had been taken, but many had been lost in the war. There were hundreds of Laura's mother and literally thousands of Laura on her parents' digital camera. So she'd set about preserving all the available letters and photos be-longing to her grandmother.

'When my father passed away, I made sure we kept all the photos of him. And all the let-ters he'd written. At the time I was studying fine art, but it quickly became clear to me that what I love—what I really love—is looking after the past. Preserving it for the future. Not everyone thinks that's important, but I do.'

When she finally finished her speech she be-came aware that Henry was smiling directly at her, in a soft, dreamy sort of way. His jaw slightly slack, his eyes focused entirely on her. It was such an intense gaze Laura didn't know how to answer it. The skin on her arms prickled and her chest warmed. His blue eyes were light, as though lit from within. The only response she wanted to give to a look like that was to kiss him. But she couldn't, so she told herself to sit back in her chair and pretend she wasn't looking at one of the most handsome men she'd ever seen.

She sipped her water and coughed. 'So tell me about your work.' Getting distressed cows out of wire fences was decidedly unsexy and she needed the heat levels of this conversation to drop considerably. Potentially to freezing. 'It can't be much fun farming in winter. It must get cold.'

Henry gave one small shake of his head. It would have been imperceptible to anyone but someone who was now achingly alert to every single movement, every blink and every breath he was taking.

'I have a friend who's a farmer,' she said and instantly regretted it. It felt strange to mention Dan to someone else.

'Oh, yes? What does he farm?'

'Sheep, mostly. Cows, I think. And apples. It must be a Gloucestershire thing.' She almost blurted out Dan's name but stopped herself. How would she explain that she didn't even know his surname. She wished she'd kept Dan's existence to herself.

Thankfully, Henry didn't ask anything more.

She was more than a little tipsy when they walked back through the moonlight to the castle and the cottage. As he told her about the unlikely matches the former dukes had made she was aware of her phone sitting in her pocket. She was also aware of the fact that she hadn't heard from FarmerDan all evening, which was unusual.

You haven't messaged him either.

'Now I know why there's a secret gate at the

JUSTINE LEWIS 85

back of the garden. So the dukes could sneak out to meet the barmaids.'

They passed the path to the castle and she stopped to say goodnight, but he kept walking.

'I'll walk you to your door.'

She was sure the castle gates had been locked and the chances of something happening to her between there and the cottage were slim to none, but she was touched by the gesture. The spring air smelt of gardenias and she made small talk about the garden as they walked along the gravel driveway to the cottage.

She unlocked the door and turned; he was still standing there, head bowed under the low entrance.

She pressed her lips together. He mirrored her action.

Oh, no.

First the possible flirting, and now this. She wanted to kiss him—there was no point lying to herself.

He wants to kiss you too.

And so what if he did?

Nothing. Absolutely nothing. Leaning into this moment would be a very bad decision indeed.

'Thanks again for a lovely evening and for showing me the village, and the pub.'

Henry reached out his right hand, but a look of confusion crossed his face and he dropped it again. He looked as conflicted as she felt and she wanted to laugh out loud, but held her giggle back.

He lifted his hand again and held it out for a shake. She took his hand. It should have been a perfectly formal gesture, but when his hand enclosed hers it was nothing of the sort. Warm, secure tingles shot up her arm and directly into her heart. His hand was rougher than hers but his grip was tender. She felt her insides melting.

Henry leant forward, just the merest of fractions, just enough to make her heart leap into her throat, but then he drew back.

'Goodnight, Laura.' His voice was rough and low and it rippled through her insides, reaching every long forgotten crevice.

Inside, fingers still shaking, she sat on the end of her bed and unzipped her boots. What was she going to do?

Last night Dan had suggested they meet. As friends. She was in his part of the country. It made sense that they should finally meet. But yesterday had thrown her a curveball. A handsome duke-shaped curveball.

FarmerDan was solid, caring and interested.

Henry was handsome in a get-your-pulse-racing-into-overdrive kind of way.

He was also as good as her employer. They had a business relationship.

Henry was a distraction.

Dan was a friend.

But what if they are the same person?

The idea still seemed impossible, the product of an overactive and clearly stressed imagination, but the coincidences were starting to stack up.

Tennis.

No, many people liked tennis.

Cows.

Ditto. There was more than one dairy farmer in the county.

It was yet another coincidence.

She wouldn't know until she finally met Dan once and for all.

She took out her phone and before she could think too closely about all the reasons why it was a bad idea she typed and hit Send.

@SohoJane: Hi, sorry about all the prevarication. I'd like to meet. I'm actually staying in your part of the country for a few weeks. Near the town of Epemere. Do you know it?

She contemplated suggesting Abneyford for a meeting, but if she was wrong she didn't fancy accidentally running into Henry and/or anyone she knew from the castle. She'd driven through Epemere on her way to Abney and it seemed lovely.

@FarmerDan: I know it well. There's a great little pub on the main street, near the park. Tomorrow?

Tomorrow? He was keen, but whether he'd remain so when she told him what she had to tell him was another thing altogether.

@SohoJane: Tomorrow would be great. Around seven?

@FarmerDan: I can't wait.

Laura was breathless as she put down her phone. This time tomorrow she would have met Dan. This time tomorrow she'd know.

She made herself a cup of tea and flicked through her phone for a while, trying, without success, to wind down after the evening, but she didn't seem to be able to. A warm shower made things worse and by the time she was ready for bed, a sense of dread had fallen over her. The feeling was difficult to explain, except that something inside her had shifted.

She knew what it might be, logically, objectively she knew exactly what it could be, but she refused to believe it. The laparoscopy should have given her a few more pain-free days per month, not decreased them.

So she refused to believe it. She climbed into bed pretending it wasn't happening. This was not happening. This was too soon.

CHAPTER FIVE

THEY WERE GOING to meet. Tonight!

In Epemere, of all places. Near his village.

Laura was definitely Jane. During their conversation at the pub the night before he had been so sure they were the same person he had almost confronted her directly.

Laura lived in Soho. Jane lived in Soho!

Lots of people live in Soho.

He didn't receive a message from Jane the entire evening when they were together.

That doesn't mean anything.

A strong suspicion wasn't the same as being sure and he had to be sure so he held his tongue.

But then, not long after he'd arrived home, he received a message.

@SohoJane: Hi, sorry about all the prevarication. I'd like to meet. I'm actually staying in your part of the country for a few weeks. Near the town of Epemere. Do you know it?

It had to be her.

You want it to be her.

Henry knew other people quite happily dated a variety of people at once. But it was different with Laura and Jane—he could see himself with either of them. He had a solid friendship with Jane and loved sharing the little parts of his day and random thoughts with her. He got along well with Laura too, though he didn't know her nearly as well. Most telling of all, his pulse rocketed when he was around Laura, his hands became embarrassingly sticky and something else came over him. An urge to reach over and touch her. To lean in and discover how her skin felt against his lips…

Even though he would be meeting Jane tonight, Henry still longed to see Laura as soon as possible. He walked through the main house, anticipating seeing Laura at the threshold of each new door. But he went through room after room, and there was no sign of her. After he'd walked through the whole house twice he asked Louis if he knew where she was, but Louis hadn't seen her all day.

He asked a few of the guides, who shook their heads as well. His heart rate kicked up a notch. No one had seen her since yesterday.

It was a Thursday, a workday, and while Laura was free to come and go as she pleased and not be beholden to a timesheet, it was worrying. Her absence didn't fit with everything he knew about Laura and her passion for her work. He needed to check on her.

He passed the lines of visitors and walked briskly to the cottage. The small red brick house looked still and the curtains were all drawn. He knocked gently and waited. He knocked again, and this time counted to sixty. When there was no answer still he knocked harder. No response. He contemplated going back to the house for the master key, but before he had to decide whether that was a good idea he heard the lock turning.

'Laura, it's Henry. Are you all right?' he said before she opened the door fully. His throat closed over when he saw her. She was drawn, dishevelled, with a thin sheen of sweat on her forehead. But it was the absence of colour from her skin that worried him most.

'I'm sorry to barge in. I was worried—are you all right?'

'What time is it?' she asked.

'It's after midday.'

'Oh, no, I'm so sorry.' Laura grimaced and gripped the doorframe, clearly in pain.

'There's no need to be sorry. You aren't well and you need to get back into bed.'

Laura didn't respond but took the three or so steps required to the nearest sofa. She sat, her face still scrunched up with pain and then lay down.

Henry's heart rate was now through the roof. She wasn't well. Not a bit.

He opened the drapes to let some light in the front rooms of the cottage. Laura wrapped herself into a ball.

'Do you need an ambulance?'

'No,' she said but it came out as a croaky whisper.

'Can I call your doctor or should I get mine?'

'There's no need,' she said, 'I know what this is, but I didn't get my latest prescription filled. This has taken me by surprise.'

'No problem—I can do that for you. Do you have a copy?'

'It's in my handbag.' She pointed a floppy arm to the coffee table. 'I thought I had another week to fill it, but obviously not. I'll be okay, at least I'll be able to stand when I've had some.'

He looked down at the script for a strong painkiller. Then he looked back at Laura.

'Are you sure you're all right?'

'Yes, well, I'm in a lot of pain so no, but it's not life-threatening. It's endometriosis.'

Period pain. Bad period pain, that's what he knew. Alarmed as he was by how she looked, he was relieved it was nothing worse. Still, her appearance was worrying.

Henry looked around the cottage. It was dark and untouched. 'Have you eaten anything?'

'No, but I don't feel like it. I'm so sorry I didn't know what time it was. I was awake half the night and then I just must've slept through my alarm.'

'Please stop apologising. Will you be all right if I leave you for a minute to get a few things?'

'I'm not going anywhere,' she groaned.

Henry first called Claudia and explained the situation. Claudia said she would bring some food there shortly. Then he got into his car and took the script into the village. He worried for a moment the pharmacist wouldn't fill it for him, but he shouldn't have. He was the Duke of Brighton—the pharmacist barely blinked. While he waited for the script to be filled, Henry looked around the pharmacy. He saw the heat packs and hot water bottles and picked up some of each. As he wandered around the shop he picked up one of everything and everything that might have anything to do with periods, not knowing what she used or what she needed. None of the staff even gave a second glance at his basket, overflowing with pads and tampons of all shapes and sizes. He threw in some jelly beans and chocolate for good measure and returned to Laura.

Back at the cottage he took the medicine and a glass of water to Laura, who thanked him again. 'Give me ten or fifteen and this will start to work,' she said. 'I may not be high-functioning, but I'll

be lucid briefly before I fall asleep.' She let out a
sad, half laugh after she said that.

He passed her the bag of supplies. She looked
inside and he could see that she was trying not
to smile.

'There's ibuprofen and paracetamol underneath
all of that as well. The pharmacist said you know
what you can take with your other medicine.'

She nodded, and he could see she was biting
back a laugh. He didn't care if his lack of knowl-
edge of endometriosis showed, he simply wanted
her to have everything she needed.

Claudia kept the place in perfect order, but
Henry thought about what he liked most when
he was unwell. He put on the kettle and when
the water had boiled, he filled the hot water bottle he'd just purchased. There was enough left
over, so he brewed two cups of tea. Laura shuf-
fled into the kitchen, wrapped in a cotton robe
and he passed her the hot water bottle. 'How do
you have your tea?'

'White with one,' she said.

'Sit down, please.'

She went back to the sofa and he brought her
the tea.

Laura sat, her feet tucked under her and her
body wrapped around the hot water bottle. She
pulled a blanket around herself and sipped the
tea gratefully.

'This is so embarrassing,' she muttered.

'Not at all.'

There was nothing to be embarrassed about, though this was one of those occasions he suspected the 'being a duke' thing got in the way of him just wanting to be a good person.

'Are you feeling better? You look better. There's a little colour in your cheeks.'

'Yes, thanks, the medicine is kicking in. Of course, shortly it'll make me dozy and I'll be out again.'

'Claudia will be here soon with the food, if you can hold out that long.'

'I'm so sorry, I didn't realise it would be so bad. I thought…' Her words lifted off. Whether it was from the pain medication or something else he couldn't tell.

'Is this worse than usual?'

'Not exactly, but it's unexpected. I had a procedure a month ago and it was expected to help avoid times like this. But I guess not.'

'Please excuse my absolute ignorance, I've never known anyone it affects.'

She looked down, looking both devastated and in pain. He knew that look. It was a look seen on his father's face in the weeks before he passed away.

Laura isn't going to die.

He knew that, logically, but the worry building up inside him felt a little familiar. And it was awful to watch someone you care about in so much pain.

'It isn't like a bad period. It's not *not* like that, but my friends get cramps that go away after some anti-inflammatories and a sleep. This is still there when I wake up and goes on for days. And it's more than just a cramp. Sometimes it feels like I'm being stabbed.'

Henry couldn't help but wince. 'And the procedure was meant to help?'

'Keyhole surgery, a laparoscopy, to remove some of the scar tissue.'

'I don't understand.'

'The lining of my uterus grows where it isn't meant to on the outside round my ovaries. My doctor has made several attempts to remove the material from where it isn't meant to be. But this can also create problems over time if adhesions grow over the scar tissue. Basically, my insides are a mess. I've also been taking hormones to simulate early menopause. It isn't great, but I'm running out of options.'

'What causes it?'

'No one knows.'

'Isn't there anything else they can do? Further surgery?'

Laura grimaced. 'There is. But it's radical.'

'Radical? How?'

'A hysterectomy.'

'Oh. That is…radical. Yes. But surely after you have children?'

She sighed. 'That's what my mother says, but the thing is that isn't very likely.'

'Why not?'

'Endo can affect fertility. And given the history of mine, it's severity and the number of operations I've already had, the chances of me conceiving and carrying a baby to term are close to nil.'

His heart broke for her. It was such a cruel, insidious disease. Not only did it leave her in excruciating pain, but to possibly cause infertility as well. It was so unfair.

Something else slowly dawned on him. If Laura couldn't have children then he couldn't marry her.

And if Laura was Jane…then neither of the two women he was hoping might become his wife could have children.

It isn't about you, he reminded himself. He stood, went to the window and looked out over the lawn. He took a deep, focusing breath.

'So then why not a hysterectomy?'

'That's what I've been saying, it does seem to be the best chance I have to be pain free.'

'Is it like this every month?' he asked, still disbelieving that in this day and age a woman had to go through something like this.

'More than not. I'd hoped that this most recent

procedure would give me a few more years to decide, but now—' she looked down at her stomach '—it doesn't seem to have made any difference. If anything, this is sooner. And worse. The plan was to see how this went and then make up my mind about the next steps.'

'You're in the process of making this decision now?' The significance of what had been going on in Laura's head all this time was only now occurring to him. Sometimes you really had no idea of the burdens other people were carrying.

She nodded. 'They really don't like giving hysterectomies to women who haven't had children and who are still in their childbearing years, but I've been seeing my doctor for a long time. I have a good relationship with her and she knows my history. The plan was to have the laparoscopy, see how it went and then wait a few months before having another serious discussion about it.

'She's not going to refuse to do it as some doctors might, but she does want me to be sure.'

Henry ran his hand through his hair. 'Oh, Laura, that's a huge thing to have been on your mind.'

She nodded. 'Yes.'

He felt helplessly ill-equipped for this conversation and for something to say. Most of his male friends didn't closely consider fatherhood, or if they did, they didn't speak about it, but he understood both the need and the desire to have children and suspected it was a feeling that was even stronger in many women, with both biological instincts and societal expectations pushing them towards it.

'Do your friends, your family, do they know?'

'Yes. My mother's been supportive, but I know that she wants me to wait a bit longer. She's convinced I'm going to meet someone.'

'But it isn't about that,' he said. 'It's about asking you to live the next few years of your life in pain on the off chance you might conceive a child, which doesn't seem very fair.'

'Life isn't fair,' she mumbled sadly to herself.

'No it's not,' he agreed, feeling the unfairness intensely himself.

At that moment there was a knock on the door and Claudia came bearing hearty soup and fresh bread. Accepting Laura's urging for him to leave and let her rest, he did, closing the door to her cottage quietly behind him.

The first thing Henry did when he got back to his apartment was take out his tablet and type 'endometriosis' into the search engine.

He was shocked to learn that it affected roughly ten percent of women globally, not to mention the life-impacting nature of its symptoms. It wasn't just painful periods, as he'd vaguely thought, but could involve chronic pelvic pain, bloating, ir-regular bleeding, nausea, fatigue and depression.

His heart broke for Laura. And all the other women affected, particularly those who could not access proper treatment or those whose symptoms were dismissed by their doctors.

Laura's endometriosis was found in the ovaries, but there were several types and several stages. The more he read the more he learnt and the sad-der he became.

And angrier.

Women were expected to carry on through nor-mal life while being in debilitating pain or being so fatigued they couldn't function. No wonder de-pression was a side effect, he thought as he read through more and more accounts.

Then he looked up 'endometriosis cure' and what Laura had said was essentially it. Pain man-agement, keyhole surgery, hormone treatment and then more radical surgery. Looking up from his tablet he realised it was late afternoon. He put it down, knowing there were things he should get on and do but at a complete loss as to where to begin.

He sighed and his phone vibrated with a mes-sage.

@SohoJane: Hi, I'm really sorry but I'll need to take a rain check on tonight. Something has come up. I'll be in touch.

SohoJane was cancelling their date.
Henry buried his face in his palms.

'Is everything okay? You didn't answer yesterday,' Laura's mother asked the following afternoon.

Laura was out of bed and had managed to shower, dress and even eat a little. She was contemplating doing some work, though Henry had told her to keep resting and not rush back when he'd dropped around more meals Claudia had prepared that morning.

But Laura felt guilty about coming all the way to Abney Castle to work on this special assignment and then being unable to show up to work. She was also feeling vaguely guilty about the amount of food that was building up in her refrigerator and worried how on earth she was going to be able to get through it all.

Henry had been letting her rest but was checking in morning and evening and using food delivery as an excuse. She was touched by his caring and generosity.

But she still felt guilty.

'Not really,' Laura said.

'What's up?'

'I've been laid up for the last two days.'

'Not with…oh, no. Already?'

'Yes. It's like the laparoscopy didn't even happen.' Talking about it now brought the disappointment up to the surface and she felt something welling up inside her.

'Oh, darling, but that doesn't mean this is how it's going to be.' Her mother, the eternal optimist. Managing to stay positive in the face of all the evidence to the contrary.

'I wish you'd told me. I would've come.'

'It's okay, they're looking after me.'

'They?'

'Claudia, the housekeeper, has been cooking for me.'

'And the duke?'

Henry had definitely gone above and beyond. It was touching, but confusing as well. They both knew now that regardless of any attraction they might share or frisson they might enjoy, they would never be more than colleagues or friends. 'He's been very understanding as well.'

'Good. As he should be. How are you feeling now?'

'I'm slowly feeling like myself again. I'll try and do a few hours work this afternoon.'

'You shouldn't rush back.'

'But I feel guilty.'

'You're allowed to take leave,' Fiona said but Laura barely listened. Her mother didn't understand that given all the time Laura had to take off she had to work extra hard to make it up to everyone. No one understood this, not her mother, or even her friends.

Fiona filled her in on her own weekend and just as Laura was about to end the call Fiona said, 'And have you been in touch with FarmerDan?'

Laura wasn't about to tell her mother her suspicions—or delusions—that Henry and Dan could be the same person. She wasn't going to tell a soul anything until she met Dan and found out one way or another.

'I'm going to arrange to meet him,' she confessed.

'Fantastic! When?'

'Soon,' Laura said and ended the call.

Now that she told her mother she'd have to go through with it.

The town of Epemere was a fifteen-minute drive away from Abney. It was the first time in over a week that Laura had left the idyllic world of the castle and the village, though driving her hatchback along the hedgerows and lanes of the picturesque Cotswolds, as the sun lit the honey-coloured stone was hardly like re-entering the real world. The directions Dan gave her were good and she had no trouble finding the town or the pub.

It had taken her a few days to get through her recent attack. She had returned to work in the castle but Henry's initial attentiveness had appeared to cool. Which was fine, she told herself, he was her employer. He had already gone above and beyond to help her when she was unwell. It would be strange for his twice daily visits to continue once she was well again.

But her worries about whether they were the same person lingered and as soon as she was confident her pain had passed she rescheduled the meeting with Dan.

They had again agreed to meet in the nearby town of Epemere. The pub Dan had suggested looked as though it was cut from the pages of a tourist guide, complete with a set of loyal locals. It was the sort of place she'd love to have as her regular. She looked around the bar for someone likely to be Dan. Or someone in roughly the right age bracket, but saw no one. She was ten minutes early. It was always difficult to decide whether to order a drink first or wait for a date to arrive.

She wanted a drink—heavens, she needed something to quieten the nerves that were conducting a gymnastic competition in her stomach—but she didn't trust herself not to slam it down in one gulp.

This is Dan, she reminded herself. The man she'd been messaging for months, who had been nothing but kind and understanding. He would be just as lovely in real life as he was online. She shouldn't feel nervous—she *knew* him.

But then she thought, *This is Dan.* The man she'd been messaging for months. The man she felt a connection to. The man she really liked, but at the same time didn't want to like too much because she had enough going on in her life already.

She walked up to the bar and picked up the wine list. As she waited for the bartender to serve another customer a jingle at the door caught her attention and she spun.

It was him.

Of course it was him.

She wasn't attracted to two men at once, she was attracted to the same man. Twice.

Relief. Pleasure. Excitement.

Her instant feelings were short-lived when she saw the look on his face. His smile was soft, almost shy. But it held no hint of surprise. As he walked across the room to the bar his face darkened, became serious. Almost businesslike.

The reality of their situation washed over her and she felt every muscle in her body sag. FarmerDan was really Henry Weston, the thirteenth Duke of Brighton. And he needed an heir. He needed a wife who could give him something she could not.

Instead of embracing one another, as she'd once foolishly thought they might, he held back, aloof. Standing stiff and shifting his weight from one foot to the other.

'Can I get you a drink?' he asked.

'Yes, white wine, please.'

The business of ordering drinks gave her a moment to collect her thoughts and lower her heart rate.

What a mess. What should have been a wonderful meeting was now high on her list of all-time most awkward first dates ever. The only consolation, if you could call it that, was that she hadn't been paranoid or mistaken—her suspicions had been spot-on. But that gave her little comfort.

He wasn't overjoyed to see her. Surely even the coincidence should cause his lips to twitch upwards. But it hadn't.

'You knew, didn't you?' she asked.

He lowered his head. 'Didn't you?'

She looked down as well. 'I suspected. I wasn't sure. That's why I asked to meet.'

Without speaking, they took their drinks from the old wooden bar and found a table in a dark, unoccupied corner of the pub. Given the weather was so warm, most patrons had chosen tables outside, but the dark secluded corner suited them best.

'When?' she asked.

'Almost as soon as you arrived.'

She could no longer stay calm. Rightly or wrongly, she was annoyed. 'You knew all this time and you didn't say anything?'

'Yes, no. I wasn't entirely sure and I didn't know what to say without being sure. I didn't expect to feel…'

That sentence lay unfinished. Neither wanted to pick it up and analyse the meaning behind it.

'I knew you weren't ready to meet me,' he continued. 'I knew Jane wasn't ready to meet Dan and I didn't know what to do. Honestly. I didn't want to lie, but I didn't want to pressure you either.'

She sipped her wine. He made a fair point and yet everything inside her still felt wrong.

'Are you angry with me?' He pulled a face so dejected she felt his sadness in her gut.

'No, I'm…'

'You are.'

He held her gaze in his. She felt his blue eyes pierce into her mind, her chest, her heart. It was almost too much to keep looking at him. Familiar, strange. Wonderful. Impossible, all at once.

Henry's expression softened and the look between them broke. She couldn't be mad at him, no more than he should be mad at her.

'No, I'm not angry,' she said. 'It's a mess, that's all. I'm sorry I didn't say anything as well.'

'No, I'm sorry. I wanted to wait for you to suggest it. I didn't know if you would ever be ready.'

That was, she conceded slowly, the truth. She'd made it clear that she didn't want to meet him and that she wasn't in the market for a relationship.

She'd also, more than once, rejected his gentle invitations for casual meetings.

'But…' she started to say.

But when you met me, wasn't it too late?

He answered her unspoken thought. 'Yes, when we met I should have said something, but I struggled and I'm sorry. I made a whole lot of excuses—you're working for me, you don't want to meet me, you have your reasons… I wasn't sure you liked me. I wasn't sure you wanted it to be me. All those excuses added up to me not telling you.'

Buried in that long list was a brief but heartbreaking reason and she didn't hear much of what he said after that.

I wasn't sure you liked me.

There was much insecurity buried beneath that comment. How could someone so handsome, charming, intelligent, impressive and downright lovely be so insecure?

'I do like you. Very much,' she said softly.

A touch of pink glowed on Henry's cheekbones.

If she didn't like him so much this wouldn't be hard. Or so confusing.

'I don't think I ever explained why I was on A Deux,' he said.

'You said it was because of bad experiences.'

'Yes, but you probably assumed I meant the same sort of bad experiences that you had. Catfish, scammers.'

She nodded.

'I had all that, but when I put my real name up, or even a proper photo, I'd get so many messages.'

'That should be a good thing, shouldn't it?'

'It should be. And I met some wonderful women. But…'

'What?'

He sipped his beer and looked around the room, even though they were on their own. 'It's hard to phrase it without sounding like a jerk.'

She reached over and touched his hand. Henry wasn't a jerk and she wanted him to know it.

'Usually around the second date they'd start to ask a lot of questions. About the estate.'

'I'm not following. I've asked you heaps of questions about the estate.'

'I don't mean the sort of questions you asked. You have a reason to ask questions. I mean mentioning things out of context. About how it's run, what sort of shape it's in. Financial questions.'

Now she was following. She nodded.

'Once or twice they asked about my family circumstances, about my father. His health.'

'Oh, no. I'm so sorry.'

'And even if they were subtle, I'd suspect that was why they'd matched with me. It got to the point where I'd simply just suspect every single woman of being out for my money and my title.

And I'm sure they all weren't, but I could never feel sure.'

She was certain there were many great women out there who would instantly see Henry's wonderful qualities without caring whether he had a title. She was one of them.

'And I might be a little paranoid after...' Henry ran his hand through his hair with so much force she was surprised when he didn't come away with a fistful. He was so nervous he was practically vibrating. She reached across the table, picked up his hand and squeezed it. If he felt the gesture was overly intimate, he didn't say anything. Laura felt strangely anchored by gripping him; the rest of the world was swirling around them—secrets had been discovered, revelations were being made. They would not be the same two people walking out of this pub as they had been coming in, but holding on to him she felt she'd know which way was up.

'When I was at university, I was with a woman for over a year. Her name was Beatrice. She was a medical student and I thought we were happy. I thought she loved me.'

His voice cracked on the last words.

'What happened?'

'I found out she was considering dropping out of her studies because she decided she was going to be a duchess.'

'I don't understand.'

'It wasn't something we talked about—I hadn't even proposed, though I was seriously thinking about it.'

'You didn't want her to give up her career for you?'

'Of course I didn't. But it was more than that. When I asked her about it she didn't understand what the big deal was if we were serious about one another. I told her I didn't expect her to give up her career, but she told me it wasn't important to her. Basically, she let me know that I was her ambition. Being a duchess was more important than being a doctor. I asked her if she'd still love me if I wasn't heir to a dukedom and she couldn't answer me.'

'I'm so sorry.'

'That's why I don't tell prospective dates. I don't want to lie to anyone, but I don't want it to be everything. Do you understand?'

Laura nodded. She knew exactly what he meant, because she knew about dating with secrets. And deal-breakers.

She always struggled to find the right time to tell a man about her endometriosis and its likely impact on her health and fertility. When she mentioned it early on in a relationship, before even meeting, the men rarely suggested a date. Sometimes she'd waited, only to be accused of hiding things. Or in the case of one very unkind man, misleading him.

'You don't want it to be everything,' she said. 'But it isn't insignificant either. It is part of who you are.' She was talking to herself as much as to him.

Henry nodded and thankfully smiled.

Why was she surprised, the one thing about her and Dan—and her and Henry now she came to think about it—was that they did understand one another most of the time.

'I thought discretion was such a good plan, but it seemed to have backfired on me this time,' he said, thoughtfully tracing the rim of condensation his glass had left on the coaster.

Laura waited for him to finish. His shoulders were falling noticeably as he was getting all of this off his chest.

'There was one more reason I didn't want to tell you who I was. An important one.'

'Yes?' Even though Henry had just opened up to her about a great deal of painful matters, she had a feeling she knew exactly what he was going to say. There was still one more matter that was unspoken between them.

'You're unlikely to be able to have children.'

'And you must have them.'

'I wouldn't put it exactly like that,' he said.

'I would. You have a family legacy to uphold.'

And apart from anything else, he probably wanted to have children because most people did. It was a biological drive, people longed to carry a baby in their arms, or hold a toddler's hand. People even wanted to steer moody teenagers to adulthood.

As the light outside faded, his eyes became darker, but no less earnest. 'I like you, Laura.'

'I like you too and having a family is something I would never want to take away from you. Dukedom or not.'

'I suspect that's why you stepped away from dating? Why you first told me you wanted to keep things platonic?'

'Yes. But for some reason we kept chatting.'

They smiled sadly at one another across the wooden table, still holding hands. Her stomach, still annoyingly melting as his blue gaze held hers. His thick brown lashes shadowing his eyes, the corners crinkled, his soft pink lips twisted into a sad grin.

'What do we do from here?' she asked.

'I don't know. But I think to start with, would you like to join me for dinner?'

CHAPTER SIX

THEY ORDERED A meal and another drink. Henry was worried the conversation might dry up, now that they had everything between them out in the open, but it was the opposite. He found they had more to talk about with one another than ever.

They both had two people to reconcile, two relationships to merge, and after the initial awkwardness, it was almost fun. They compared notes openly and honestly about their first connection, and then the first meeting at Abney. She still laughed about the calf and what a mess he'd been. By the time they had finished eating he could hardly believe he'd ever thought Laura and Jane were two different people.

He wasn't sure what made him open up so honestly with Laura, probably simply the fact that he had always talked so honestly with Jane. He hadn't expected all the stuff about Beatrice to come tumbling out, but, he realised they really were friends. After this conversation they could be nothing else and he didn't want to lose her from his life. They might not be able to marry or have a relationship, but that didn't mean they couldn't be friends. Nothing had to change, did it? They could keep messaging on another; the only thing that would change would be that they would use each other's real names.

When they left the pub, it was still twilight and Henry led Laura around the laneways of the town, of which he was familiar and she was not.

'Why is all the stone around here so beautiful?'

'It's the fossils. From the Jurassic age. The Cotswolds were over a hundred million years in the making.' His family only went back a fraction of that, but at times it felt as though it didn't make any difference. That they had lived here for ever.

'Tell me honestly,' he asked. 'Why did you keep messaging me after you said you were stepping away from dating?'

'I… I guess… I liked you. And you seemed to understand. Even though you didn't know what was wrong, you understood.'

'I had no idea what it was, I thought you might have a family member who was sick or dying. Or something like that.'

'Because of your father?'

'Probably. When he was dying, dating was the last thing on my mind. I stopped for over a year. I only got back onto A Deux after very sustained pressure from my mother. It's strange—once I inherited the dukedom the pressure on me to marry really kicked up—but it was, at that time, the absolute last thing I wanted to do.'

'And now?' she asked.

It was difficult to answer her.

'Dating is still the last thing I want to be doing.' But now the reason was different. Laura and Jane were the only women, or rather, the only woman, he'd felt any connection with in the past year, but she was not his future wife.

'But you have to.'

Did he? He supposed he did. But it would be nice, if just for this evening they could forget about the future and just concentrate on getting to know one another, face-to-face, with no secrets between them.

'Why did you choose SohoJane as your name?'

'Jane's my middle name and I live in Soho—no other mystery. And you?'

'I'm a farmer and my middle name is Daniel.'

'Henry Daniel,' she whispered.

'It's a family name, it was my father's name as well.'

He didn't mention his brother.

They drove back to Abney separately, as they had come. Henry insisted Laura follow him but made sure she was following close behind as she wasn't as familiar with the roads as he was. She parked at the cottage and he pulled up his car nearby and walked over to her.

What should have felt like a hello had the heavy weight of a goodbye. He'd anticipated this moment for so long, part of him had been hoping that whatever it was that was keeping SohoJane away from meeting him would resolve itself—hopefully in the happiest way possible—and that she could see a way through to meet him. To be with him.

And once he'd met Laura, yes, he had hoped they were the same person, not simply because the coincidences were so numerous, but because he wanted them to be the same person.

And they were.

And everything should have been perfect.

But of course it wasn't.

They met at her door. She turned to him and a small line creased her forehead between her eyes. She released a sigh that he felt in his gut. 'It's such a shame,' she said.

'I know.' Because they both knew a future together wasn't in the cards it felt safe to also admit, 'I really like you.'

'I really like you too.'

He wanted to step into her, let her embrace him, to feel her arms around him, to feel her body against his. To comfort one another. But sensibly she stepped back.

'Friends?'

'Of course.' Was that ever in doubt? Maybe it was. Maybe a friendship would complicate things; maybe she wasn't ready to label this thing platonic and carry on. Maybe he wasn't either. His heart still raced a little too fast when their eyes met; his palms sweated a little too much.

'Goodnight,' she said.

'Goodnight. And Laura, despite everything, I still am so glad we finally met.'

The smile she returned didn't reach her eyes.

Laura flopped on the soft sofa, spread her arms wide, and let out the groan she'd been holding in for the past few hours.

Far from being delighted that Henry and Dan were the same person, now everything between them was as tangled up and confused as peak hour traffic in London.

The only thing she knew for sure, the thing she had to keep reminding herself, was that no matter how rapidly her pulse raced when she was around him, she and Henry would only ever be good friends.

Friends isn't nothing.

But friends wasn't enough when all she could think about when she was with him was sliding her hand around his waist and her tongue into his mouth. Friends in circumstances like that would be nothing short of torture.

Her phone pinged. It was probably her mother and she should get breaking the news to her out of the way.

Yes, Henry is Dan, but he's the last in a long line of dukes and the thing he needs most of all is the thing my messed-up womb can't give him.

But it wasn't her mother. It was Dan.

Henry. You need to remember that he's Henry Weston, the Duke of Brighton, and all the baggage that comes with that and he's not just your easygoing online friend.

@FarmerDan: Hey, how you doing?

@SohoJane: I had a rough first date tonight.

@FarmerDan: Oh, no, me too. Wanna talk about it?

Talk or cry, she thought. But instead she wrote:

@SohoJane: I was really looking forward to meeting this guy, and he was as wonderful as I'd hoped.

@FarmerDan: Yeah, I know what you mean. Fate is fickle.

Exhausted but still knowing it would be a while before sleep claimed her, Laura found her limbs positively itching to do something. It was getting dark, but the grounds of the castle would be safe. If she could just work off some of the excess energy coursing through them she might be able to sleep.

She took off her boots and replaced them with her runners. Then she grabbed her phone and keys and set off quickly to catch the last of the light.

But when she opened the door, there he was. Looking at his phone, but still standing where she'd left him less than ten minutes ago.

Henry turned at the sound of the door and his eyes met hers, loaded with want. She knew what it was because she also felt it in her gut. She stepped towards him and before she could think twice she did what she'd been wanting to do for days; she slid her hands around his waist and lifted herself up onto her toes to meet his full pink lips.

Henry froze for perhaps half a beat, surprised no doubt at her lack of ceremony, but then she felt it—his arms, his hands, his strong hard body, and at the centre of it all, his lips, which met hers like they were made for one another. Relief and release wound through her in happy spirals, his tongue sliding against hers, cautiously at first, then deeper, wider, like his arms, that reached around her, holding her tight and close and matching her want, stroke for exquisite stroke.

It was illicit, dangerous and the most perfect kiss she'd ever had. She wanted to keep climbing into it, to lose herself in his arms for ever and never have to face what waited for her on the other side.

But eventually she felt his arms slacken and felt his breaths mix with hers. Panting, he pulled slowly back.

'Friends don't usually do that, do they?' he asked.

'Not all friends. We might need to come up with our own idea of friendship.'

His body was still pressed against hers, feeling quite unlike any other friendship she'd had in the past. She felt his inner turmoil each time his hard chest rose and fell against hers. She wanted him. She needed him like she needed air.

'Maybe,' he said and with that, the spell was broken, the mood shattered. Laura pulled away, extricated herself from his uncertainty.

She'd overstepped, badly. Embarrassment, desire rose up inside her, threatening to break over her face.

'Anyway, goodnight!' she said as cheerily as she could.

'Laura, wait. I don't know what's going on between us—I don't know if kissing you is a good idea.'

She nodded. 'You're right. We talked about this. I'm sorry.'

'No, we didn't, not really. Not properly. Laura, I don't think kissing you is a good idea because I don't know if I can stop.'

Ah, her thoughts exactly.

Did they have to stop?

Laura imagined five minutes into the future, taking his hand in hers, pulling him wordlessly into her cottage and closing the door behind them. Maybe she'd lead him down the hall to the bedroom. Maybe they wouldn't even make it that far. Maybe their knees would buckle on the living room floor as their need and want consumed every breath they had. One thing was certain, that if he came inside with her now she also would not be able to stop. Not tonight. Maybe never.

He wanted her as much as she wanted him, so one of them had to stay strong, because Henry Weston must not fall in love with her.

And most importantly of all, she must not fall in love with him.

'You're right.' She nodded slowly, taking a further, safer step back, out of his warmth, out of his reach.

'I want to,' he began.

She waved her hand up to indicate that she understood, her throat suddenly constricted, her mouth now incapable of making a sound.

'Goodnight, Laura Jane.'

'Goodnight, Henry Daniel,' she managed before fleeing inside, with the door safely between them.

By the time Henry was up, dressed and about the next morning he still hadn't figured out what had happened last night. The facts were clear enough: his suspicion was correct and Laura was Jane. It was so obvious he could hardly believe he'd doubted himself. The relationship he had with Laura was so similar to the one he'd had with Jane: an easy, happy understanding and a conversation he never wanted to end.

But, instead of being glad that the two women with which he had this amazing connection were one and the same, instead he knew they didn't have a long-term future and their relationship must remain a friendship.

Except that once they had spoken about all of this and agreed, she'd kissed him.

He'd been waiting outside her cottage, his feet unwilling or unable to take him home, and then there she was, coming outside and kissing him and he'd kissed her back like his life depended on it, because for those few stolen minutes it had. His lips still throbbed, and other places besides, at the memory of her body in his arms and her mouth on his.

Where did that leave them? The same place as it had before the kiss—absolutely nowhere, but twisted up in it.

There was some small chance Laura could conceive, but not only might it take a long time and a lot of assistance, while she waited to conceive she'd be in pain. He couldn't ask her not to get any treatment she needed; he couldn't watch her be in as much pain as she had been last week—that was out of the question.

They had to remain as friends only and that was better than nothing. They didn't belong together and this evening he'd take her up the hill and show her why.

At around 5:00 p.m., the time FarmerDan would usually message SohoJane, Henry made his way through the house where he found a few staff members helping Laura lift a painting back onto the wall. There was much laughing and a light-hearted banter between Laura and the others and Henry held back for a moment watching her. Her long hair was tied back, but loose strands had escaped their bindings and fell into her face. She wore overalls over a white T-shirt, her usual work attire. But she didn't look usual to him today. She was SohoJane. And Laura. She was impossible, but no less lovely, he realised with a pang.

He had to take her up the hill because then she'd understand. And when she understood she'd realise why he couldn't keep kissing her, as much as he wanted to.

Henry cleared his throat to gently let the others know he was there. The mood shifted slightly, as it often did when he made his presence known. There were nods and 'Good days,' but then everyone left him alone with Laura.

'How are you feeling?' The question was loaded with too many implications and he quickly added, 'Physically.'

She smiled. 'I'm okay. Physically.'

'You're taking it easy though, aren't you?'

'I'm fine, really. I bounce back quickly.'

'But still, you should look after yourself.'

'Aye, aye, boss.' She was smiling.

He was stalling and they both knew it.

'I was thinking, I still owe you a tour of the monument. Up the hill.'

A long beat passed and he could see her thoughts ticking over. Weighing up the fact she wanted to go with the doubt as to whether it was a good idea.

'I'd like to show it to you.' This was the truth. So far he'd told her a little about his family, but once she went up there, she'd really know.

She nodded. 'Yes. That would be great.'

'This evening?'

'Yes, please.'

By the time he knocked on the door to her cottage, with Buns and Honey eagerly at his heels, he was excited to be seeing Laura but wondering at the same time if he was being a fool asking to spend more time with her. How could they just be friends if every time he anticipated seeing her his heart rate ran a little faster?

Because when she sees what is at the top of the hill she'll get you. The monument at the top of the hill, or rather what was inside it, could explain Henry Weston to Laura better than any words he could come up with ever could.

Laura was wearing jeans that fit her shapely body snugly and a soft white sweater. The spring evening had a slight chill to it, but it was clear and perfect for a walk around the castle. Her long hair cascaded down her back in dark, silky waves. As they made their way across the grounds and up the gentle hill, he couldn't stop thinking about running his fingers through it, but evidently Laura's mind was more safely occupied. 'Why isn't it open to the public?' she asked.

'A few reasons. It's special to our family. But we've also set it, and this entire area aside as a protected wildflower sanctuary.'

'Why is that?'

'Most of the wildflower meadows in the country have been lost over the past century, so to preserve and regrow them we, along with many others, have set aside land for the meadows to grow wild.'

The hill was dotted with blue and purple flowers. There were dogviolets, pasqueflower and cornflowers the colour of Laura's eyes. Butterflies danced over them. The dogs raced each other along the path.

He unlocked the gate and Laura entered first. As they climbed the hill to the monument, the wild, overgrown nature reminded him of the length of time his family had lived there and his responsibility to them. When they approached the summit the path gave way to stone steps. At the top, there was a three-hundred-and-sixty-degree view of the countryside, taking in the entirety of the castle's grounds, their village and several more besides.

'Wow. It's amazing,' she gushed as she caught her breath.

'And if you come over here, you can see all the way south down the valley, across three counties.'

Laura stood where he motioned and he watched her shoulders sag as she exhaled and took in the view. The sun was low in the west, bathing the whole place in a honey-coloured light. The ruins, the house and the villages glowed in the sunset.

'It's so beautiful. Thank you for showing me. It's a shame others don't get to see it.'

'Yes, but it's also important to have areas like this left as they are. Preserved for the future.'

She smiled softly and gently touched his forearm. 'Then I'm very thankful you showed me.'

The touch of her hand made something in himself melt. Resisting the urge to pull her to him he said, 'Would you like to see inside?'

'We can go in? I'd love that.'

He held up the keys and led her over to the double wooden doors.

The room was always lighter than he expected; apart from a few stained-glass panels, the circular building appeared to be windowless, however, once you were inside you realised that a circle of windows at the bottom of the dome gave the room all the light it needed. The three stained-glass panels cast the occasional rainbow.

Laura sucked in a breath and whispered, 'It's beautiful.'

He nodded. The architect who had designed this space over two hundred years ago had been inspired.

After admiring the ceiling and its dome, Laura made her way slowly around the room. 'Oh, Henry. There are graves.'

He stood back and watched her look, a lump rising in his throat. He'd only ever known one of the people lying here. The twelfth duke. His father. Yet he knew the names on all the plaques.

She turned back to him, eyes wide. 'I'm so sorry, I didn't realise it was a mausoleum. I assumed it was simply a folly.'

Henry nodded. Most people did—after all it looked like a small Greek temple, just as all the other eighteenth-century follies of the time did.

'It was a folly, at least once. The sixth duke built it in the eighteenth century for his wife, but she loved it so much she asked to be buried here. Ever since then, every duke and his wife have been interred here.'

Laura spun and stared at him, her jaw slack. 'And your father?'

He nodded.

Laura met his gaze and held it, wordlessly acknowledging his loss. 'Would you mind showing me?'

Henry walked over to the place, though as the newest, shiniest plaque it was easy to spot. It read:

John Daniel Weston
Twelfth Duke of Brighton
Dearly loved, terribly missed
Son, husband and father
Honour, faith, love

He heard her draw in a deep, serious breath. 'Tell me about him.'

'My father?'

She nodded.

Why did he struggle to describe him to Laura? The plaque said all the important things; he was a son, a husband and a father and he was loved. And missed. 'He was my father, and he was wonderful. He adored me and my mother, and he loved this place. He devoted his life to Abney Castle and the people of this region.' As he opened his mouth to say something else his throat closed over and from nowhere he felt something well behind his eyes and nose. He swallowed it back.

She smiled softly. 'I miss my dad too, and it's still hard to talk about him. Even after all these years.'

Henry wanted to step closer to her, pick up her hand and squeeze it, to comfort her as much as himself, but he remained rooted where he was, his chest tight, emotion unexpectedly threatening to break through the surface of the careful calm he was trying to maintain.

Laura didn't push her comment further and walked sombrely around the room. There was no rhyme or reason to where his ancestors were interred. Many were under the ground, some in the walls.

'The ninth duke. Tell me about him.' Laura

pointed to a bust of a moustached man on a pedestal. One of the largest and most ostentatious monuments in the room.

'Well, his wife is over there.' Henry pointed across the room. 'As far away as she could be from him.'

Laura laughed. 'Yet they are both here.'

'He spent a lot of his time in India. She spent a lot of hers with one of the stablehands. And this was their son, the tenth duke.'

'The one who married the gardener's daughter?'

Henry paused, amazed at her memory. 'The very one. And the tenth duke had ten children, or rather, his poor wife did. Apparently he was very proud of the fact.'

Laura grimaced, as well she might.

'And this is the sixth duke and his duchess, Frances. Together.' He pointed to the marble slab that marked their resting place.

'It's a lovely stone.'

Unable are the loved to die
For love is immortality

Did love that strong really exist? If it did, it was so rare. He understood, maybe for the first time in his life how lucky two people were to find love like that. Until now he'd taken it for granted. His parents had loved one another deeply. As had his grandparents. But what if that was not going to be his fate? He was thirty years old and yet today he felt further away from it than ever.

Laura stopped in front of the next plaque, as he'd hoped she would.

'Daniel Weston,' she said and touched her fingers gently to the dates. Then she looked at him, her face creased with questions.

'Was he your brother?'

Henry nodded.

'But he…'

'Yes. He died before I was born.'

'Oh, Henry. How old was he?'

'He was seventeen. It was a riding accident.'

It was strange to tell this story because it wasn't exactly his story. Even though, were it not for the accident, he, Henry Weston, would not exist.

'Your poor parents. He was their only child?'

'Until then, yes. They…well.' Henry looked at the stone floor. 'After he was born they tried to conceive again, but they couldn't. They weren't overly worried. They had an heir after all. But then my brother died so they had to try again. But this time with assistance.'

'IVF?'

'Yes. It took a while, nearly two years, but they got me.'

'How old was your mother?'

'She was forty-three when I was born. It was a high-risk pregnancy, she was on bed rest for the last two months and she nearly died giving birth to me, but…' He didn't want to speak for either of his parents; he knew the sacrifices they had made for him. His mother had been forty-three when he was born but his father had been fifty. Henry knew he'd had a different upbringing to his older brother.

'It would have been so hard for both of them. So hard for her,' he finally said.

Laura turned her back and stepped away from Daniel's plaque. 'Is that how the Weston women are meant to be? To go to all those lengths to provide an heir?'

'No, that's not it at all. I would not expect my wife to go through what my mother went through just so there could be another duke.'

'Then what do you mean?'

He scraped his fingers over his scalp. 'My parents went to a great many lengths to have me. The entire reason I exist is so I can be the duke. It is my sole destiny. I can't just ignore that.'

'I'd never ask you to give that up. I do understand.'

'Do you?' His voice cracked across his throat.

'I do. I do understand…really, I do. And honestly, it wouldn't have mattered to me if you were a duke with a title to bequeath or just a man who wanted to be a father—I'd never ask anyone to give up something like that.'

He believed her—she was Jane. And Laura. Laura Jane. There were few people in the world he'd ever trusted more.

'That's why I stepped back from dating in the first place. But you…'

'I didn't listen.'

'No, that wasn't what I was going to say,' she said with a grin. 'I didn't follow my own advice either.'

They faced one another, just a few feet apart. Their bodies pulling together, but the weight of the history in the room pushing them apart.

'Let's go, that is if you're ready?' she said.

He nodded. He'd had enough of the Weston family crypt for one day.

'Graveyards always make me philosophical,' she said.

'Not sad?'

'Not exactly. They remind me that life is finite and that makes me remember to treasure every day and strangely that makes me happy.'

'I don't think that's strange. It means you're remembering to be grateful for the life you lead and that's always a good thing.'

She was amazing… She held so much goodness within her. But the more he found to like and admire about her, the harder things became.

His mind leapt back to how she'd been last week when he'd found her unwell, ashen, sweaty, her face creased with pain. She'd been enduring that sort of physical misery regularly for years.

'How do you manage to stay so upbeat, so grateful after everything you have to go through?'

Laura regarded him, temporarily lost for words, and then looked at the ceiling. 'I guess when I'm in pain, I remember that it will pass.'

'And when you're not?'

'I try to focus on the here and now. I try my best not to think too much about the future.'

He led the way outside, surprised by the light; the countryside still glowed like golden honey.

Laura waited a few steps away while he re-locked the door.

Be grateful for the life you have. If he could just keep remembering that then it might be easier to keep Laura at a safely platonic distance.

They didn't speak on the walk down and Henry's thoughts kept coming back to his father, his brother. All the dukes resting at the top of the hill. With their devoted duchesses. And the not so devoted ones.

Would that be his lot? To be buried across the room from his wife like the ninth duke?

Or would she be like the wife of duke number six and lie for eternity with her husband? Would he be like duke number ten and sire ten children. He shuddered. That did seem unlikely.

Had any of them worried about the things that he worried about? His father had, certainly, but the others? Had they worried about the future in the same way that Henry did? Constantly and fearfully?

Laura waited for him at the gate at the foot of the hill. It was unlocked, but he held it open for her. When she walked past him their arms brushed against one another's and his entire body flooded with warmth and sparks and every muscle in his body waited, as though they all knew that being next to Laura, touching Laura was their one true purpose. Laura paused as well; the warmth from her body spread into his, the gentle friction between their bodies only exciting him more. A brush wasn't enough. He needed all of her.

He leant in. When he was this close to her the rest of the world dropped away. Became an insignificant afterthought. Laura let out a half sigh, half groan and his insides flipped. Pleasure laced with desperation. Was that how she'd sound if he was holding her, properly and forgetting the rest of the world existed? Should he live for the future? Or should he live for the here and now? No one knew what the future held.

'They remind me that life is finite and that makes me remember to treasure every day.'

'I don't know what to do,' she whispered. 'I don't know why it's so hard.'

'Because we like one another. It was always going to be hard.'

'I don't want to lose you from my life, but I don't know how to do this. I don't know how to be near you without wanting to do this.' Laura lifted herself and her lips found his. He could taste her wanting because he felt it too. She was there in his arms but would never be his. He stepped back before he tasted too much more and was lost for ever.

The trip to the folly was meant to help, it was meant to put something between them, but instead it had only seemed to bring them closer than ever.

I try to focus on the here and now.

Maybe his problem was that he was focusing too much on for ever when he should just be focusing on here and now?

CHAPTER SEVEN

'CAN I BUY you dinner?' Henry said as he stepped away from another almost kiss, leaving Laura struggling for breath and composure.

The entire evening had been moments of 'almosts'. Almost hugging him when he spoke about his father, almost pulling him to her when he read her the inscription on the plaque marking the spot the duke and his wife were buried together.

Now at the gate an 'almost kiss'. She'd brushed her lips against his but instead of doing either of the two things she'd expected, kissing her back or pushing her away for good, he'd asked her out to dinner.

'Is that a good idea?'

'You've been to the village pub, it's pretty good.'

He knew what she meant, and he'd dodged her question neatly, but she took his point. He was offering her dinner, not a night of passionate lovemaking. Dinner and probably a drink. That was all. He was being the sensible, rational one, whereas she was in turmoil.

Why was it so hard? She'd had male friends before, even ones she'd been attracted to, but it had never been like this. Her body had never felt so torn in two.

The dogs came with them to the village. The four of them sat at a wooden table outside, Honey and Buns sitting at Henry's feet as though they were accustomed to the routine. They ate and drank in the setting sun. He insisted she try the local cider, fermented in his distillery, which was pleasantly dry and refreshing. Henry waved and nodded to the locals, some of whom stopped for a quick chat, careful to acknowledge Laura without appearing too curious. Henry's explanation that she was an art conservator working for him a few weeks elicited warm smiles. Henry was easy with the locals and they were with him. The brief conversations ranged from wool prices to the upcoming village fair. He was less lord of the manor and more respected colleague, neighbour and friend.

This only made her ache further. Couldn't he have at least one downside? A single red flag? Some flaw, however minor, upon which to hang some hesitation.

But no.

Henry was lovely.

Quite possibly perfect.

But he wasn't perfect because he wasn't perfect for *her*. How was she meant to carry on a platonic friendship with him when every cell in her body wanted to throw itself at him?

It was dark by the time they left the pub though and as they made their way back, she lost track of the path, veering into the grass. Henry was far more familiar with the route than she was and grabbed her arm to set her straight. But once she was back on the path he didn't let go of her arm. Instead he linked it through his and they continued to walk, arm in arm, warm body against warm body, along the path and through the castle gate.

She liked it. No, she adored it. Henry's body rubbing against hers was perfection, but it was also sending her thoughts into overdrive. This was how the almost kiss at the gate had started—they were veering into dangerous territory.

Yet she was helpless to remove her arm from his.

'Can you…' he began after a while. He cleared his throat, his voice raw, he began again. 'That is… I've been doing some reading on endometriosis. I know it's more than simply bad period pain. I know it can have all sorts of other effects.'

'Yes, but pain is one of my main ones. Bloating sometimes and nausea, but it's the pain that's the biggest problem.'

'Does it affect any other activities?'

'Like work?'

'Yes, that but other physical activities.'

It took her a moment to gather his meaning and when she did, her heart missed a beat. 'Are you asking if I can have sex?'

'I wasn't going to put it so unromantically.'

'It's not unromantic to talk about it.'

'Then, yes, I guess, I was. I don't want to ask you to do anything that is painful. I don't want to hurt you. I want to understand how it affects you and what I can do for you.'

'What I can do for you.'

Laura's heart leapt into her throat, almost cutting off her airway. Her body rippled with sparks.

You can carry me to my cottage, rip my clothes off and touch, stroke and kiss every single inch of me, quickly, then slowly, and then quickly all over again. You can do anything you want to me provided I can do the same to you.

But, breathless and barely able to keep walking, let alone speak, she didn't say that out loud.

'And by answering that question, that doesn't mean I expect...'

This man.

She stopped walking and squeezed his arm. When she'd calmed her excited body and caught her breath she spoke, 'It doesn't hurt, not usually. I enjoy it, as long as I'm not in pain otherwise.'

When she was in the middle of an attack, intercourse was almost the last thing on her mind. But when she wasn't, sex could be wonderful. Especially when she was with someone caring. And if she was with someone like Henry then it might be amazing.

'We're clearly friends who like to kiss. We could see if we could also be friends who like to have sex.'

'And…'

'And…do we need to know anything else? Can we not think about next week, or even tomorrow?' he asked.

'Most relationships don't last…they burn themselves out or end anyway. So we shouldn't be putting pressure on ourselves,' she agreed and felt a weight lift from her shoulders. She was overthinking all this, when really the answer was simple: make the most of life. Live for the moment. At any time either one of them might end up in the grave. Of course hers wouldn't be in a Grecian temple on a hill overlooking three counties in the Cotswolds but the end result was the same.

'We're making this more complicated than it needs to be,' she went on.

'I agree—it feels like a lot of pressure not to give into something we both want.'

'Oh, yes,' she said, exhaling.

They didn't say much more as they walked the

rest of the way back to the castle, but their pace picked up considerably. There was something exhilarating about knowing what they were about to do.

Sex. They were going to have sex. The anticipation alone raised the hairs on her skin, the fizz under it.

Her heart still beat in her throat and she stole glances at him in the increasing darkness, could make out the silhouette of his beautiful jaw, sometimes glimpsing a smile on his lips which only made her chest burn more.

'My room or yours?' he said as they approached her cottage.

'Yours. No mine.'

'There are twenty bedrooms here.' He grinned. 'Or anywhere else you'd like.'

'Mine.' This time she was sure. She felt more comfortable there and, more importantly, it was closer.

He stood a foot or so behind her as she unlocked the door, but she felt him anyway. She stepped back to let him and the dogs in first and then shook as she shut and locked the door behind them. Honey and Buns gave a cursory glance around the cottage, as though it wasn't their first time visiting, and then both sat obediently by the unlit fireplace.

'Will they be okay?' she asked.

Answering her question themselves, the dogs lay down and sighed, tired after their long walk.

Henry smiled at her, but the adrenaline or the nerves, she wasn't sure which, rose up inside her. She started to fuss around the room checking windows, closing curtains, which was entirely unnecessary, but the anticipation was so overwhelming she didn't trust herself not to fall apart.

She'd wanted this since the first time she saw him in real life, and probably before that as well, if she were being completely honest.

'Is everything okay?' he asked softly.

'It's great.

'Exciting?'

'You have no idea.'

'Try me.' He smiled again and this time she noticed the muscles around his eyes quivering. He was struggling as much as she was. 'Show me where your room is.'

'You know where it is.'

'I want you to show me.'

She nodded and led the way down the short hall to the room she'd been sleeping in. He kept a few feet between them, both knowing that once they touched stopping would be next to impossible, engulfed by a passion that neither would be physically or emotionally able to quell.

Henry stood a foot away from her and a smile grew slowly across his lips. She shifted her weight from foot to foot, knowing she was teetering on the edge of a cliff, but also knowing that all she had to do was take a step forward and she would be caught.

By the time they finally came together she wanted everything at once. She pushed her body towards him, opened her mouth wide and started tugging at his shirt.

Henry was having none of it. He took her shoulders and held her at a short distance.

'Slow down, please.'

'Slow?'

'Please. I want to remember this. I want you to as well.'

'How on earth do you expect us to slow down?' she gasped. She wanted him yesterday. She wanted him last week already. Slow down? It would be easier to stop a runaway train.

'Lips only,' he whispered and lifted his hands from her shoulders. Their eyes met and she blinked in agreement, her entire body buzzing. He leant forward and touched his lips gently against hers. She opened her mouth as slowly as she could, savouring each movement, each breath, each stroke.

Slowly at first his tongue began to explore her mouth and she let hers wander. Every ounce of blood in her body flooded to her lips, every other cell screamed with jealousy.

Half opening her eyes she realised that Henry was tilting slightly; she wasn't the only one struggling to stay upright. She pulled back and grinned.

'Tops only,' he conceded.

She groaned but didn't need to be told twice. She pulled his shirt from under his belt, then, as she caught her breath she unbuttoned his shirt, carefully, deliberately.

'I'm not going anywhere.'

'No, because you're a giant tease, Henry Weston.'

She felt his gorgeous lips curl into a smile as he pressed them against hers again and her heart felt like it was melting. She was going to be a puddle on the floor at the rate they were going.

Moving back and catching her breath, she decided to give him a dose of his own medicine. She spread her fingertips over his chest as she pushed back his shirt, examining every inch of him, the lay of his muscles, the pattern of his veins his alert nipples, his firm chest covered in a smattering of hair.

Then she walked behind him and did the same to his bare back—slowly traced the lines between a few random freckles, watched his shoulders rise and fall with each rough breath. She spread her hands over his bare back, feeling the muscles she'd been admiring for days, exploring his arms with her fingertips, his neck with her lips.

The air in the room was so charged she wouldn't have been surprised if she'd seen sparks flicker in the air.

'My turn.' His voice was hoarse as he turned and stilled her gently. He slipped the fingers of both hands in hers and time stopped as she watched both their hands entwine and dance together. Then he took the hem of her shirt between his fingers and lifted it over her head. He repeated her ritual, explored the sensitive bare skin of her shoulders, her chest and her back. His lips made a pilgrimage down her body, to the edge of her bra and traced the line between her breasts. Finally she felt his fingers push the annoying fabric of her bra down and as the clasp released he gave an audible sigh.

She looked into his bright blue eyes now darkened with desire. She stepped back towards him but he gave his head a quick shake and nodded to the bed.

Thank goodness. She was shaking so much her knees were about to give way.

He pulled her to the bed and she waited, stretching across it, every one of her pores crying out to be touched by him. He lay on top of her, warm torso to warm torso, and his lips made their way slowly over her neck and back home to her own mouth.

His groin pressed against hers, and any desire he might have had to keep their bodies apart was now abandoned. Hard and persistent, she reached for his belt, but just before she claimed it he shifted his weight, lowered his head and took one of her nipples into his mouth. The tension that had been coiling inside wound even higher and she saw stars. 'You do realise that will almost be enough to break me, don't you?' she said, panting.

'That's my aim,' he murmured as he licked her again, his lips making their way from one aroused breast to the other and then lower, to her waistband, where he paused and looked up at her. Laura was desperate to get out of her underpants but just as desperate to get him out of his. She shook her head. 'You first.'

Henry rolled over dutifully. She ran her hand over the front of his jeans, saw his eyelids lower and could tell, finally, that his resolve was breaking too. She unbuttoned his jeans and pulled them down slowly, so that every movement was a caress. She ran her hand over the front of his pants, feeling him hard and ready under the thin fabric.

He gave permission with a grunt and she grabbed his waistband, dipped her hand beneath it, grasping his long, full length, feeling him shiver.

'Damn.'

'What?'

'Do you have protection?'

She didn't. 'I'm healthy and we both know pregnancy isn't on the cards and the drugs I'm taking make it impossible.'

'I'm healthy too. But do you want to be sure?'

'I'm sure if you are.' She rubbed his length, which was hardly conducive to good decision-making, but she didn't care. If they only had this short time—if they only had this one time—she wanted them both to enjoy it as much as they could.

She kissed his cheeks, his neck, collarbone, breathing in the delicious smell of his skin, that was heightened by the warmth of their bodies against one another's. His lids lowered and he nodded, grabbing her again and pulling her close.

By the time he entered her she could hardly see straight from longing. His strokes were long and certain; her entire body ached and clenched for him. He reached parts of her that she'd only reached in her dreams.

She nearly lost her mind. The climax when it came was even shocking in its intensity. She felt every one of his sighs in her gut.

'Henry,' she cried and felt him shuddering. The world slipped away for a moment and slowly came back together. He held her close, both panting, gathering their breath.

When she opened her eyes the world looked

different. Something had shifted. Months of tension had been released, but there was something else.

A new weight. A new reality.

Was it possible? Had she been this careless?

Not to sleep with him without protection, but to sleep with him at all? Could she simply sleep with a man like Henry and not start to fall for him?

Laura slid out of her bed and into the bathroom.

Henry rolled onto his back, spread out his arms and moaned softly.

He was in big trouble.

He was going to remember this night for the rest of his life. Nothing, or rather no one, would be able to come close to making him feel what Laura just had.

Laura was amazing, but he felt that he'd put on an exceptional performance too. He'd never been so motivated, so desperate, to please someone in his life. She made him a better lover. Thirty years old and he'd just had the best sex of his life. Except that…he looked at the closed bathroom door. What was she thinking behind that door?

He'd suspected that sleeping with Laura might not be the most sensible idea he'd ever had, but he hadn't expected it to be this problematic. He hadn't expected to see colours he'd never known existed. He hadn't expected everything to shift so significantly.

He had foolishly hoped that his desire for Laura might fade once he gave in to it. He hadn't even imagined that his desire could only grow. This evening, as they ate and talked, he thought he wanted her as much as it was possible to want a person. But almost as soon as they'd come together he realised that everything that had come before was only the beginning. Like an addict, now that he'd had a taste he only craved more. To the exclusion of everything and everyone else.

He breathed in deeply.

Get a grip.

This was simply the afterglow of an amazing lovemaking session talking. Once he left, went out into the rest of the world, he'd see sense.

Pain healed. Hurt faded. He knew that. He'd got over women before; he'd moved on, life had returned to normal. And after Laura left, things would return to normal again. But was he just supposed to turn this off now? Not spend time with her, simply because it might hurt when she left?

It was already too late for that. They might as well make the most of things while she was here. Like she'd said, most relationships don't last, they burn themselves out.

The bathroom door clicked and Laura emerged

wearing her robe and chewing absentmindedly on her thumbnail. He noticed the exact moment she realised what she was doing and she pulled her hand quickly from her mouth. 'You're welcome to stay, but I understand if you'd rather go back to your own bed,' she said.

Was she saying she didn't want him to stay in her cottage or was she as self-conscious about this moment as he was?

'Is it a problem if I stay?'

'No, not at all. Just in case you'd be more comfortable in your own bed.'

'The only way I'd be more comfortable in my bed is if you were with me.'

Her shoulders dropped and she sat on the edge of the bed, exhaling.

'You're wondering what now?' he guessed.

She nodded.

'Me too.'

He liked that they were so honest with one another and talked so openly about what was going on. It made things easier.

'That was…'

She nodded again. They were both there, it was clear to anyone in the room that something pretty wonderful had just happened.

'Pretty good,' she said after a moment.

'Pretty good? Do I need to try harder next time?'

She stifled a laugh. 'If you can do better, I'd like to be there.'

He picked up her hand. 'You're only here for a few more weeks. It'd be a shame not to live in the moment for a little while longer. To see if I can't do better than that.'

He held his breath while he waited for her to answer. If this was their one time, if he never got to hold her again, then he wasn't sure how he'd manage to be around her for as long as she was working and living here without wanting her.

'It would be a shame. I think I'm going to take my own advice and live in the moment. The future will take care of itself.' She leant down and kissed him gently, sealing their promise. 'You should stay,' she said. 'Do you want another drink?'

'Are you having something?'

She smiled. 'What I'd really like is a cup of tea.'

He laughed. 'That sounds perfect.'

She brought the cups back to bed where they sipped them and lay together, chatting just as Dan and Jane had each evening. About everything and nothing.

When their cups were drained she looked at him. He stared into her eyes, feeling as though he'd known her for ever. She grinned and moved towards him.

Pleasure tumbled through him again as he felt her weight press deliciously against his and as her lips sought out his. Her pressure soft at first, but the kiss opened and deepened quickly and naturally.

Her skin was like silk against his fingertips, her warm body pliant and soft in contrast to his own which was suddenly hard, alert and ready again. When they made love a second time it was no less earth-shattering than the first, maybe more so as he was finding the places she liked to be touched, learning the rhythm she needed.

He needed to please her, to pleasure her. He wanted to make her happier than she'd ever been before, but he didn't know why. And he didn't want to know.

Live in the moment.
The future will take care of itself.

CHAPTER EIGHT

LAURA'S PHONE RANG just before she was about to get into the shower after work. She glanced at the screen.

Mum.

Laura hadn't been actively avoiding her mother, but she hadn't been rushing to return her calls either. If she didn't speak to her mother soon she'd be bound to send out a search party.

'Darling, you're a difficult girl to get a hold of.'

'I'm sorry, I've been busy.'

'Good, I was worried you were sick again.'

'No, I've been fine.'

Laura sat, untied her shoes and put her phone onto speaker mode.

'What's been keeping you so busy then?' Fiona asked.

'This and that...'

Spending every spare moment I have with a handsome duke. Last night he picked me up in his light blue Aston Martin convertible and we drove through the hills to Cheltenham for an amazing dinner. The night before that we made love in his bedroom with the huge French windows wide open and the smell of the spring garden floating. This morning he mentioned taking me to Paris for the weekend so we can visit the Musée d'Orsay. He says that it's work related, but we both know it isn't and would probably be breaking all the rules we silently set for ourselves.

But she didn't mention any of that.

'How's the work going?'

'Good. It's going well. The paintings are wonderful and thanks to the way Archibald and the family have looked after them, they're in very good condition.'

'So you'll be home soon?'

'We'll see.' Laura wasn't taking any more time with the work than she ordinarily would, though she wasn't rushing to finish it either.

She had to tell her mother. If she didn't and she somehow found out, Fiona would make it into a bigger thing than Laura wanted it to be.

'And, look, please don't get excited, because it isn't anything serious, but I've been going on a few dates.'

'With the duke?'

Despite Laura's warning, Fiona's excitement almost caused Laura's phone to vibrate.

'Yes, and Dan.'

'You've been dating both of them?'

'Sort of. They are the same person after all.'

Laura braced herself for more squeals over the phone line but none came, which was even more ominous.

'How? I mean…how?' Fiona asked finally.

Laura gave her a brief run-down of her suspicions, Henry's behaviour when she was unwell, her suggestion they meet and then the date at the pub in Epemere. By the time she'd finished, Fiona wasn't squealing any more, she was subdued.

'So, that's why I told you not to get so excited. It's just a temporary thing. Just a bit of fun while I'm here, that's all.'

'But, darling—'

'But nothing, Mum. I thought you'd be happy for me.'

'I want to see you getting out, having fun, but I don't want to see you heartbroken.'

'I won't be, Mum.' She would be sad when she and Henry parted, but she'd gone into this with her eyes wide open and she was keeping her heart locked safely away. She knew as well as anyone this was a temporary thing and they had both decided to simply enjoy the time they had together.

Fiona let the subject drop. 'What are you doing tonight?'

'A quiet night by myself.'

'Really?'

Fiona wasn't usually a judgemental mother and

she probably wasn't being one now, but Laura was unsettled. She was reading things into her mother's remarks that were not there or at least unintended.

'I've a lot of television to catch up on.' And sleep too.

Henry was busy with the final arrangements for the village fair that was coming up in two weeks' time, on what would probably be Laura's last weekend at Abney. The Dukes of Brighton had been hosting an annual village fair for over two hundred years. There was a small but active organising committee, of which Henry was the chair. Each fortnight he attended a meeting with the committee, but now that the fair was nearly here, the frequency of the meetings had increased.

'You should come up and visit. I'll only be here for another fortnight or so and the Abney Fair is happening in two weeks.'

'You want me to meet him?'

That wasn't exactly the piece of information Laura wanted her mother to take away from the invitation, but it was out there, nonetheless.

'I want to see you. And I'd love for you to see where I've been living and the castle. And yes, you'll meet Henry too, but please, don't read any-thing more into it than that.'

'Of course. I'd love to come. I'll be there.'

After saying goodnight to her mother, Laura

made herself a light dinner and flicked through the television several times, looking for something to watch, but nothing seemed to quite match her mood. Happy, but on edge. Content but anticipatory.

She couldn't help but think of Henry, meeting the committee at the village pub, finalising the last-minute details. There would be over a hundred stalls, many from local producers, food vendors, as well as animal displays and children's activities.

His work on the committee energised him. She could see how much he loved this part of his job. He wasn't annoyed by the minor frustrations and setbacks that occurred as a part of organising an event such as the fair, but rather revelled in helping others, finding the humour in everything.

She was just thinking about pulling up off the sofa and taking herself to bed when her phone buzzed with a message.

Henry: Are you still up?

Was this what she'd been anticipating all evening?

Henry arrived, barely five minutes later, with all the appearance of having walked very quickly back from the village.

It was impossible not to smile at the red-faced

and slightly dishevelled man who walked across her threshold, his blond hair slightly askew. The brightness in his eyes lit the fire in her belly.

He slid his arms around her waist and she stood on her toes to reach his lips.

Their kiss was tender, adoring, but slowly moved deeper. His tongue explored her lips and mouth, searching, probing and she opened her mouth and her heart to him.

'Hey,' he said, pulling back after a while for air.

'Hey, there. I didn't think I'd see you tonight.'

His face clouded over. 'Is it all right that I'm here?'

'It's more than all right—it's a wonderful surprise.'

Henry exhaled.

They undressed one another carefully, taking their time to kiss and stroke each new inch of skin as it was revealed. Sometimes they rushed, as though they had only minutes left, sometimes, like tonight, they took their time, pretending, she thought, that they really did have for ever. Kissing every inch of one another's bodies, exciting every pore, and making sure no part remained unexplored, untouched or unloved.

After, as they lay together, he told her about his evening, making her laugh with stories about the organising committee, a diverse group of people of all ages and by the sounds of things the only thing they appeared to have in common was that they were as devoted to bringing the fair together as he was.

Her heart swelled at the love he had for his community, for the work they were doing, making people happy, supporting local businesses and making money for charity to boot.

Henry loved his village and his community.

Be careful.

It was one thing to live in the moment and ignore the future, but the more she got to know him the more her heart grew for him. She had to keep reminding herself to hold that part of herself back.

She yawned and rolled to the side, feigning exhaustion and hoping that sleep claimed her quickly before he said anything else. Not only did she have to keep her heart safe, but she couldn't let Henry risk his. She cared for him too much to let him jeopardise his future. Sleeping with one another might be harmless fun, but by spending time with her Henry wasn't spending time finding the mother of his children.

The best way to keep your heart safe is to make sure his does not belong to you.

It was exceptionally bad timing that the lead-up to the annual fair was in the same few weeks of Laura's visit. At other times of the year he had more free time, but this was one of the busiest times of year for him. The fair had several official organisers, but they had reached the pointy end where everyone had to pitch in. Dukes included. It was the biggest day of the year for the village and the castle—they spent all year planning it in one way or another. It was fun to organise—even with the inevitable setbacks—and he always felt an immense sense of achievement watching everyone enjoying themselves. He'd been taking on more organisational responsibility for the last few years, as he had gradually with many other tasks as his father's health declined. His mother was also expected back, but this was a slight source of worry. His mother, Caroline, would be bound to meet Laura.

What if his mother didn't like her?

No. The idea was preposterous. How could anyone not love Laura?

Not that he *loved* her as such. That would be foolish. They were enjoying her time at Abney for the next couple of weeks, but they both understood that their relationship had an end date. It was unspoken, but implicitly agreed, that once Laura had finished her work at Abney she would return to London and their relationship—at least their physical one—would end.

The physical distance between their homes had never struck either of them as a barrier; she travelled around the country for her work; he visited

London regularly. Both had begun their time on A Deux looking for matches in a large geographical area. If they wanted to keep seeing one other after she left Abney they could make it work...

But he reminded himself, it didn't matter if they *wanted* to see one another after she finished her work at Abney, they had tacitly agreed *not* to. Their entire fling was predicated on an agreement that it must be temporary.

But it was now Saturday night, and he just wanted to put that all to one side to spend the rest of the weekend with Laura. She'd met him in the village for a drink and dinner and they were now strolling slowly back to the castle and what he hoped would be an evening of languid, luscious lovemaking.

'Are you still on the app?' Laura asked out of nowhere as they were walking through the back gate to the castle grounds. Her tone suggested she intended the question to be light, casual. Almost as though she was asking him what he thought of the weather, but it stopped him in his tracks.

'A Deux?'

She shrugged.

He spluttered. 'How can you ask that?'

'I was wondering. We're friends still, aren't we?'

'Yes, of course we're friends but...' They were so much more as well.

He had to get married if he wanted a legitimate heir to carry on the title—there was no other option. But now that he imagined himself opening up the app again, swiping through the photos for a prospective duchess, his gut clenched. And not in a good way. In an I-might-just-lose-my-dinner-in-the-nearest-bush kind of way. Dating someone else would be like cheating on Laura. Marrying someone else would be worse. How could he do that to Laura, let alone his poor wife, whoever she might be?

'I'm not on that app. Or any app. I haven't opened a dating app since you arrived here. And I have no immediate plans to do so.'

Laura nodded and pursed her lips together but he got the impression the conversation wasn't over, just put on ice.

Hours later, after shedding their clothes, their inhibitions and the awkwardness of their earlier conversation, Laura sat on his couch, wrapped only in one of his shirts, sipping a glass of cognac, an after-sex ritual they seemed to have adopted. They had a routine. They had rituals. They were a couple, whether she wanted to admit it or not.

'So, do you happen to have plans the weekend of the Wimbledon final?'

'Why?'

'I have tickets. I thought we could make a weekend of it.'

Laura's body stilled. The room seemed to go silent as if even the frogs croaking outside the open window were judging his comment. 'That's months away.'

'Yes, but they're difficult to get.'

It was difficult to get tickets unless you were a duke with a long connection with the All-England club. She didn't answer him, and he didn't press. Instead they talked about the fair, the dogs, the ordinary minutiae of his day that he'd become so used to sharing with Laura.

He was up, pouring himself another drink and telling Laura about Natalia, one of the castle guides who also helped with publicity for the fair. Natalia had managed to get a video of some newborn lambs playing with some eight-week-old puppies advertising the fair to blow up on social media with well over a million likes.

'It was great advertising, but I'm not sure we can handle thousands more people turning up next week.'

Laura laughed. 'Relax, the video of the lambs and the puppies was gorgeous—you might get a few extra visitors, but I don't think you'll be overwhelmed with people. Natalia is great.'

'Yes, and a good employee.'

'She's single,' Laura said looking into her cognac.

Henry's jaw locked and he could only mutter, 'What do you mean?'

'Only that there are lots of eligible women out there.'

'You're trying to set me up with Natalia?' His tone was furious, but he couldn't help it. He felt like she'd just pulled his heart out. And then looked at it with disdain.

Natalia was nice, but he'd only ever seen her as an employee. How could Laura even think he was looking at Natalia as a prospective future partner?

'I…um…' Worry creased Laura's beautiful brow.

'You're wearing nothing but one of my shirts and telling me to date other women?' Aware that every cell in his body was vibrating, Henry stepped toward the windows and took some deep calming breaths. The conversation was very close to running dangerously out of control.

Are you angry at her, or are you angry at yourself? Are you upset because you know she's right? Because you know, deep down, that what you and Laura are doing right now is reckless and has been for some time?

Laura pulled the shirt tighter around herself. 'It's what friends do, isn't it?'

He stopped himself just in time from saying, 'But we're not just friends,' because it was his silly idea to call this thing they had between them friendship.

He sat next to her, the anger dissipated. He only felt tired.

'Laura, tell me. What's going on?'

'I've been distracting you from doing what you need to do and I feel guilty about that.'

'Guilty? Why?'

'Because, for months now you've been messaging me when you should be meeting other women, and now we're spending all this time together when…'

'I'm with you because I want to be with you. I'm not waiting for something better to come along.'

'But that's the thing, you *should* be.'

'I'm confused.'

'You should be looking for someone else.'

'I don't think I've ever heard you so down on yourself. What's the matter?'

'I'm not down on myself. I'm really not. I've always accepted who I am and what my body is and isn't capable of and I've made my peace with it. Honestly.'

He nodded. She was one of the strongest, most self-possessed women he'd ever known.

'It's nothing like that, but exactly what I said. I've been distracting you from what you need to be doing.'

'You want to stop…this? I don't, but if you do…?'

She spoke softly. 'I don't want to stop. I just always assumed that when I finished work here that it would be over, but now you're talking about Wimbledon. That's months away.'

'Ah, I see. You don't want to see one another at all afterwards?'

'Afterwards.'

Afterwards had once seemed like a theoretical time, in the long distant future, and the rules of afterwards had never been clear.

He assumed it would mean their physical relationship would end, but everything else? Their friendship? The thought of losing that made him hollow. They had been friends for far longer than they had been lovers.

'Whether you want to talk about it or not, it's going to happen. You're going to date someone else. Marry someone else. And I'm okay with that. I understand that. I understand that our time together is finite.'

'But will we still be friends, afterwards?' He hated asking the question, but dreaded her answer more.

'Your wife may not like me. She may not like the idea of us remaining friends.'

'I'm not going to marry someone who doesn't

like you, or who doesn't want me to be friends with you.'

Laura smiled, but the serenity of her smile broke his heart.

'That's sweet, but don't you think that expecting your wife to be happy with a past lover hanging around is a little bit insensitive?'

He was quiet.

'Who are you going to marry?' he finally asked.

'Oh, I don't know. But I'm not on a timetable. There's less at stake for me.'

'How can you say that? Your happiness is as important as mine.'

'Yes, but it's different and we both know it.'

He was helpless to show her she mattered; she was important. Just as important as he was.

She can't give you the one thing she knows you need.

He hadn't thought this through—it wasn't meant to be like this. He hated the way he was making her feel. But he couldn't change it; it was his birthright, the very reason for his existence. He couldn't change it because it was the one thing he had no control over whatsoever.

And he hated it. He hated his title, his inheritance, his duty in a way he never had, even for a moment, before. Because of the way it was hurting Laura. The way it was tearing them apart.

'You are enough.' It was all he could say, because what else could he say?

'I know that.'

'Do you?'

'I do.'

He brushed his lips against her, tasting her, smelling her, savouring every pore, every scent. It was Laura who deepened the kiss, pulling him towards her. He could feel the desire in her and was powerless to stop himself being pulled along with it.

She wrapped her legs around him, pulled him tighter and he was helpless to let go, even though the only thing settled between them was that their bodies fitted perfectly together. She branded him with her fingerprints, delicate horseshoe shapes from her nails imprinted all over his body. She kissed him with her lips, tattooing herself across his heart.

There was nowhere else in the world he'd rather be.

Sunday was like any other workday for him, but it wasn't for Laura. And given the number of days she had left in Abney were likely limited, he intended to do the absolute minimum required of him today and spend as much time with Laura as was physically possible.

Last night's discussion was now pushed to the

far recesses of their consciousness, like a bad dream. They were both naked, their ideal state as far as he was concerned. His eyes could enjoy the sight of her soft curves and strong limbs and his skin could luxuriate in the feel of her against him. Her warm shape pressed against his, with nothing to constrain or limit his reaction to her.

Bliss.

He lay on his back, Laura rested her chin on his chest and they looked at one another, making lazy conversation, exchanging dreamy happy noises and just generally forgetting the rest of the world existed. He ran his fingers through her dark hair, like a thick comb, hypnotised by the way when it slipped through his fingers he could see strands of gold and silver reflected in the sunlight.

'What would you like to do today?'

'Do you have much work to do?'

'Nothing I can't delegate. There's another meeting, but that's just to check in later this evening. We could go for a walk or we could play tourist somewhere else. Castle Combe? Chedworth?'

'Oh, I'd love that.'

'We could have lunch. Come back for an afternoon nap?'

Her eyes twinkled. She knew he wasn't anticipating sleep.

Laura shifted off him. 'Tea?' she asked.

'I'll get it.'

'No. Don't you dare move. I need to get up anyway and I expect you to be right there when I get back.'

'Just like this?' His arms were spread, his body entirely exposed.

'Just like that.'

He was entirely at her mercy and he felt himself rouse again just in anticipation of what would happen when she returned.

She slipped one of his shirts over her shoulders but wore nothing under it and did not button it up. He watched her leave, appreciating the view of one bare shoulder and her long smooth legs as she walked out of the room.

He hoped they had moved on from her doubts the previous evening. Yes, they both knew their arrangement had a shelf life, but he couldn't believe she'd think he was considering dating other women. His head and his heart were full of Laura and he was not thinking about the future. He was doing what he'd promised himself he would do: Live in the moment. The future would take care of itself.

The next thing he heard was Laura scream.

CHAPTER NINE

HENRY LEAPT OFF the bed and rushed to the living room, realising too late that he probably should have thought to dress. Or at least grab some fabric to cover himself. As it was, his mother saw more of him than she had since he'd been a child. Shocked, she covered her face with her hands at the same moment Henry covered himself with his.

'Mum! What…?'

Laura at least had his shirt to cover herself though their current state left Caroline Weston in no doubt as to what had been happening in the bedroom.

'I sent you a message that I was on my way, though I can see you've been—' she peeked a glance at Laura from behind her hands and added '—busy.'

'Mum, this is Laura.' Henry almost removed his hands from where they were hiding himself to motion in Laura's direction but returned them to his groin just in time.

'Your Grace,' Laura said. 'Lovely to meet you.'

'Why don't I make you that tea I believe this young lady was on her way to prepare?' his mother said. 'And why don't you two get dressed?'

Despite his protests, Laura slipped out and back to her cottage as soon as she was dressed. It wasn't necessary that she leave and it made their whole situation look more casual than it was, but she insisted. 'Catch up with her, call me later.'

Henry threw on some shorts and a T-shirt and joined his mother at his kitchen table minutes later, reeling from the sudden change in the direction of his morning. He took a sip of the tea, scalded himself and placed it back down.

'Careful, it's hot. She didn't want to stay?' Caroline said.

'No, um. She had to get on with her day.'

'Really? It looked as though you both had your day planned already. The next few hours at least.' His mother grinned.

'Yes, well.' Henry looked into his tea.

'Why so coy? Tell me about her.'

Tell me that it's serious between you. Tell me that you're about to propose and that I can expect grandchildren within the year.

'She's the new art conservator they sent to replace Archibald.'

Caroline's face widened with delight, as he knew it would.

'She's been staying here for the past few weeks, in the cottage, and we've been getting to know one another.'

'Getting to know one another well by the looks of things. You worked fast.'

'It's a funny story, we'd actually already connected on the dating app I'm on, though we'd never met. And she's doing an amazing job here, she's so passionate about her work and the paintings and the whole castle really.'

Caroline's expression melted from delight into utter dreaminess. 'You really like her, don't you?'

'I do, but...'

'But what? Why does there have to be a "but"?'

'Look, Mum. We're not serious about one another.'

'Is she not serious about you?'

'Why do you say that?'

'Because, darling, your affection for her is written all across your face. Your skin changed colour when you started speaking about her, your eyes literally brightened.'

It wasn't his place to tell his mother about Laura's condition, so he didn't. He couldn't.

'We both like one another.' A lot. 'But we've agreed that this is only temporary. For while she's staying here.'

Last night he'd made the mistake of mentioning seeing one another after Laura's return to London and it had backfired. The memory of that conversation still pressed painfully against his ribs.

'But why? Where does she live?'

'London. Soho.' His tongue stumbled over the second word.

'Then we're practically neighbours.'

'But I don't live in London—I live here.'

'The distance between London and Abney is hardly insurmountable.'

If only the length of their commute was their biggest problem.

'If you want to move into Brighton House for a while, let you have some more space in London, I'm happy for you to do that. I've been thinking of spending a stretch of time in France. Or maybe Italy…'

'No, Mum, that's not it and not necessary.' If he suggested to Laura that he was going to spend more time in London to be closer to her she'd pack her bags immediately.

'It wouldn't be a problem. It's your house.'

He hated when she spoke to him like that. As far as he was concerned, Brighton House belonged to his mother. The castle belonged to a vague entity he called 'his family.' None of it belonged to him. Not properly.

'Mum, you will stay there. I will stay here and the week after next Laura will go back to London and that will be it.'

* * *

Laura's phone rang as she was dressing after her shower. It was her mother.

Did mothers have a secret code?

'What are you doing today?' Fiona asked.

Until an hour ago Laura's single plan had been to spend as much time as possible horizontal with Henry.

'Not sure yet. Henry and I were going to spend the day together but…'

'But?'

'But his mother just arrived. Unexpectedly. And now I think I'll do some work.'

'Did you meet her?'

'Yes, but—'

'Wonderful! What's she like?'

Laura could picture her mother sitting at her kitchen table leaning closer over her phone, which would be in speaker mode, expectantly waiting for Laura's answer.

'She seems fine.'

'Fine?'

Fine was as much as Laura was going to commit to at this stage. Shocked, surprised, certainly. But not quite warm and welcoming. At some point Caroline was bound to become outright hostile at the idea of a woman who had no intention of marrying her son monopolising so much of his time.

'It wasn't an ideal meeting.'

'What happened?'

'Well, we were both as good as naked, so there was that.'

Fiona laughed and laughed. 'Oh, darling, she's seen it all before.'

That wasn't Laura's hesitation. It was that Henry's mother saw instantly how involved they were. Henry's mother *must* disapprove of her—Laura was the woman who was disrupting all of Caroline's attempts to set Henry up with a suitable duchess.

Laura was a lot of things: she was smart, capable, talented and kind. But she wasn't duchess material. Laura changed the subject.

'And how was your date?'

'Oh, lovely, but he's getting very serious.'

'That's good, isn't it?'

'No dear. He wants us to be exclusive.'

Laura pulled a face, not for the first time glad her mother didn't like to video call.

'And that's a problem because?'

'Because I have a date with Tony tomorrow night and I like him as well.'

Oh, to be this sanguine about relationships.

'Mum, were you this… I don't know…this relaxed about men when you met Dad?'

'Heavens, no. I was very caught up on everything.'

'What changed? How did you get to relax about it all?'

'Oh, I don't know. Time, I think, is the only thing. I'm not looking for someone to spend the next fifty years with so the stakes are different.'

'But you still want to find love?'

'Of course I do…but, Laura, what's going on?'

Laura felt her insides welling up. The temptation to blurt everything out to her mother was suddenly overwhelming.

'Are things not going well with Henry?'

'No, I mean, yes, they are going well. And that's the problem.'

'Ah, I see. Look, chances are it will burn itself out soon anyway. Burn bright and fast, don't they say?'

Laura murmured agreement, hoping her mother was correct. They were certainly 'burning bright', but she and Henry so far showed no signs yet of burning out.

Laura passed Natalia in the corridor and her gut churned with regret. She'd suggested Henry go out with her. She'd practically suggested he marry her. Was she out of her mind? Henry seemed to think so, judging by his reaction to the suggestion he date anyone else. Or go back on A Deux. The conversation had become far more serious than Laura had intended, but when they'd made love everything had seemed so unimportant. It always did; when she was in his arms the rest of the world faded away.

Wasn't Henry the one who insisted they were just friends to begin with? He was the one who had told her it was temporary. *Wasn't he?* Laura was having trouble remembering what either of them had said, that day in the wildflower meadow. So this morning, after the argument, after making love and especially after his mother, she wasn't sure where they stood, only that something had changed. Had they grown closer? Or further apart?

Laura climbed on the stepladder to reach the top of the canvas, a two-metre-high painting of Venice by Turner that was one of the centrepieces of the collection. She hadn't yet moved it from its position in the main gallery, hoping that wouldn't be necessary. Two years ago, Archibald had taken it down and cleaned it extensively. So far its condition looked excellent, the frame, which was less than twenty years old, also showed no signs of damage. It was a magnificent painting and she was always relieved to find works such as this so well taken care of. That was one thing about the Duchy of Brighton; it took great care in preserving its legacy.

Behind her, Laura sensed the air in the room shift. She felt the people stop moving, silence fell.

Laura turned her head, and nearly overbalanced. Louis was standing with Henry's mother. 'Your Grace, this is Laura Oliver. The conservator who has taken over from Archibald. Laura, this is the dowager duchess.'

Once she regained her balance, she made her way down the ladder. At least she was dressed this time, though her overalls were still not as chic as the stylish blue knee-length dress Henry's mother was wearing.

'Your Grace, hello.' Laura held out her hand, not acknowledging their earlier meeting, though the dowager duchess did not either.

'Call me Caroline.'

'Caroline, nice to see you. Would you like to see what I'm working on?' Laura said for the benefit of the small group of staff watching them.

'That would be lovely.'

'As you know, this is a Turner from the mid-eighteen thirties. It was reframed several years ago and cleaned extensively two years ago and you will be glad to know that it still appears to be in excellent condition. I will get some help to take it down shortly so that I can examine the back and be sure, but my first impressions are positive.'

'Lovely.'

'It's a beautiful piece, as you know. From his second visit to Italy.'

As Laura spoke she got the impression from

the way Caroline kept diverting her gaze that she was only listening to be polite.

'And that's all,' Laura said, to wrap things up. She could talk about Turner for hours. 'Unless there's anything else you'd like to know?'

'Laura, you must need a break. You're already working on a Sunday. It really is above and beyond. Would you like to have afternoon tea with me? Maybe we can talk more about your work.'

Laura looked down at her outfit, stained overalls and a faded T-shirt.

'Don't worry about that. You must know by now we don't worry about such things here,' Caroline said.

Laura took a moment to tidy up her things then followed Caroline through the castle and back to the family rooms. Afternoon tea had been Caroline's object in seeking her out all along. Laura half hoped that Henry would be joining them, but she gathered by the way they walked in silence through the castle, Caroline just half a step ahead of Laura, that Laura was being led to the principal's office for a talking to and she was not at all surprised to see that Henry would not be joining them.

He had probably already had his talking to this morning.

It's just afternoon tea with your employer. You can do this.

She'd been through far worse interviews.

And besides, Laura had no intention of stealing Henry, of diverting him from his duty. Caroline had nothing to be angry about.

Caroline had a set of rooms close to Henry's but entirely separate. Claudia was waiting for them but after nodding to Caroline and smiling at Laura she disappeared, leaving behind an afternoon tea spread laid out like they were at high tea in an upmarket hotel.

She's a duchess—did you really expect a packet of assorted creams?

They made small talk about Laura's job, family and the weather before finally Caroline started to come to the point.

'I see you and Henry have hit it off.'

That was one way of describing it. 'Yes.'

'He says you both have a lot in common and he's glad you were chosen to replace Archibald. He says you're a very impressive woman.'

Laura couldn't be sure if Caroline was paraphrasing, but her chest warmed at the compliment, nonetheless.

'I'm glad Archibald chose me as well. I've enjoyed getting to work here. And getting to know Henry.'

Laura looked at the woman, in her seventies but made of steel. She'd lost a husband and a son and made goodness knew how many sacrifices to have another. Laura didn't want to upset her, but she didn't want to lie either. 'What else has Henry told you?'

'This and that. He seems quite serious about you.'

'Oh, I don't know about that.'

Carline raised an eyebrow. 'You're not serious?'

'No, I mean yes. I mean I care about him a lot.'

Caroline smiled, relaxed back into her chair.

'But neither of us are wanting to commit at this point.'

'I guess it's the fault of the internet.'

'What is?'

'Your generation.'

Laura's hackles were up at the mention of intergenerational divide.

'The apps you use, they give you so much choice you don't know what to do with it. Always waiting for something better to come along.'

'It isn't like that.'

If she met a thousand men none would be as wonderful as Henry. Laura began to suspect that Henry hadn't actually told his mother much about her at all.

'I know committing is hard, it takes a leap of faith, and heavens, being a duchess isn't about the jewels—it is hard work. But a strong friendship is the best basis for a marriage.'

Laura chewed on her sandwich far longer than

necessary, allowing her thoughts a moment to re-calibrate. Now that she thought about it, Caroline didn't seem as disapproving as Laura had expected. In fact her hesitant manner might also be interpreted as nervousness. Caroline was trying to persuade her into a relationship with Henry, not chase her away.

'It isn't that,' Laura said.

'Then what is it?'

'I'm not sure what he's told you about me, but I don't think he's told you everything.'

Caroline put down her tea.

Laura took a deep breath. 'I have endometriosis.'

'Oh, I'm sorry.'

'It's unlikely I'll ever be able to have children.'

Caroline shook her head. 'There are all sorts of treatments available now.'

'I know, but none are a guarantee. And it's more than just that. The treatments that I need now are the type that would make it difficult, if not impossible to conceive. But I want to reassure you, I know how important the title is to him, and he and I have no intention—' Laura didn't get to finish.

'I expect he's told you about Daniel.'

Laura nodded. 'I'm so sorry for your loss.'

Caroline's hand fluttered to her throat and she

looked out the window into the distance. 'Do you know what's funny?' she said after a while.

What on earth could be funny about the situation?

'I never really had a chance to mourn Daniel. It was awful, of course it was, but it was so soon afterwards that I had my first specialist appointment. I made the appointment even before the funeral. You're probably horrified, but I had to. For the family's sake.'

Laura hadn't the faintest idea what to say, so she let Caroline speak.

'When we married, I promised my husband we would be partners in the whole enterprise. And yes, running a duchy is an enterprise, make no mistake. It's as though you are in charge of a company. You own it, but really you're just holding it on trust for the next generation. It has a life, an existence, that is separate from any person. It should outlive us all.'

Laura nodded, now fully understanding Caroline's point.

'Do you care about the past? About tradition?' she asked Laura.

'I care about it very much. My job is art conservation, but it isn't just paintings I want to see preserved, it's all kinds of things. I do value your family history, which is why Henry and I...well, we care about one another, but we both know it will be short-lived.'

Caroline smiled gently. 'The treatment wasn't fun, I'm not going to lie, but it's far better now than it was thirty years ago. But it can still be an emotional and physical rollercoaster and you should know that going in.'

'Henry and I…' She started to say, *Henry and I aren't about to get married*, but something made her stop. 'I'm not going down that path, it isn't an option for me. For either of us.'

'We did try for other babies after Daniel, we never really stopped trying. It wasn't as though we gave up, so each month, although I'd be hopeful, I'd try not to get my hopes up. Sometimes I'd be so sure, I'd have a feeling that this was the month. It wasn't just about a spare, in fact it was hardly that at all. I wanted a sibling for Daniel, I wanted to feel the warm weight of another baby in my arms. I wanted a daughter.'

Laura's throat closed over.

When Caroline said that Laura also felt the sensation of holding a child, and the subsequent, inevitable, sense of loss.

'But then each month I'd get those familiar pains and I'd realise yet again that it wasn't to be. But then we lost Daniel and it wasn't enough simply to hope. I had to get assistance. And it took years—they were the worst two years of my life. First losing Daniel, then the treatment and so many disappointments. And once I was pregnant it wasn't over, then I worried about whether I'd be able to carry him to term, worried about all the things that could go wrong. The birth was difficult…and so on.'

Caroline's entire story was horrible—from feeling pressure to keep having children to provide a spare. The years of trying and failing. The worry. Then the unthinkable, losing their one son. Only to be thrown headlong into years of fertility treatment.

Why on earth would she share this story with Laura, if not to scare her away?

'What I'm trying to say is that the treatments are better now, the doctors are good. And the earlier you get started the better. If I can get pregnant at forty-two, you surely can.'

Oh, no. Caroline wasn't trying to scare Laura away, she was trying to get her to endure years of pain, treatment after treatment.

'The technology is so much better now.'

But was it really? In so many respects Laura would be in no better position than women from hundreds of years ago, expected to bear her husband an heir. If she stayed with Henry she'd feel the weight that had been on hundreds of royal and aristocratic women over the ages to make their body do something they had absolutely no control over. And while she might not be blamed these days for not conceiving, carrying and giving birth to an heir, she'd still feel something else.

Expectation.

Hope.

Pity.

She'd feel pressure.

It was bad enough her body didn't work, but to have everyone know and look and judge. Even their hope and pity would be too much.

'Caroline, I'm sorry, but I don't think the treatments today are even good enough to help me.'

'Nonsense.'

'I'm on drugs to simulate early menopause. The next step for me is probably a hysterectomy. But I want to reassure you I know how important your family is to you and I'd never ask Henry to do something to jeopardise that.'

As Laura spoke she realised the lie she'd been telling herself.

Because she was. By being with him, by distracting him, she was preventing him from finding the person he was meant to be with.

'Henry and I have an understanding,' Laura said.

'I'm sure you do. All I'm saying is don't close your mind to possibilities.'

Laura considered trying to convince Caroline that her mind was not for changing, or taking the approach she took with anyone who tried to interfere with her choices about her fertility and her body: telling them it was absolutely none of their business, but Caroline was Henry's mother and indirectly her employer, so Laura just nodded and crawled deeper within herself.

She wasn't the right person for Henry. He deserved someone who could give him what he needed. He deserved someone who could give him the world.

Laura made polite small talk with Caroline before she said she had to get back to work. Caroline promised the three of them would have dinner together at some point and Laura agreed at the same time thinking up ways she could avoid it.

She was relieved to get out of Caroline's apartments and back to work, though instead of going back out to the public areas and the Turner she went to the privacy of her workshop, relieved to be able to put the conversation with Caroline out of her mind and be alone for a while.

What had Caroline told her that she didn't already know? Assisted fertility treatments were hard and very often heartbreaking. They messed with your body and they were emotional torture.

With no guarantees.

The one thing Henry's mother had let her know was how important it was to her that Henry settle down with someone. And soon. She should have felt honoured that Caroline thought that she, Laura, would make a good duchess, but another thought kept rising to the top of her consciousness like an annoying itch she couldn't scratch.

You're not good enough for Henry.

You can't give him the one thing he needs.

Ever since her endometriosis diagnosis Laura had been aware that her fertility was unlikely to be high. Or even in the normal range. Each time she'd had every one of her keyhole surgeries to remove the lesions, she'd been warned that there was always a risk of further damage. As her condition developed she knew, without even being told, that her chances of conceiving naturally decreased every year. Assisted treatments were unlikely to be an option, her ovaries were so scarred by previous lesions, she was unlikely to have viable eggs. But she refused to feel that there was something wrong with her.

She was not her condition.

It was something she had to manage, but it wasn't her. It didn't make her any less of a person. It didn't make her broken.

And she'd never thought anything else.

Until this afternoon.

Until a woman she hardly knew implied that she needed fixing.

Something inside Laura—the stubborn, determined side, the side that had pushed her to achieve in her life, the side that had propelled her through her studies, through work, through her father's illness and death, hardened and said, *No. You are not going to beat me or break me.*

But the other side of Laura—the tired, the aching, hurting part—just wanted to lie down, curl her body around a pillow and then cry a little before sleep claimed her.

For a while the determined part of Laura pressed on, slowly and carefully cleaning the canvas, brush stroke by careful brush stroke. But when she dropped the brush for no apparent reason, Laura knew she'd had enough.

She longed for her own bed. And not just in her cottage, but back in Soho. Where her room was never entirely dark and the hum on the streets helped to distract her from the even louder hum of her own thoughts.

She sent Henry a message:

I'm not feeling well and I'm going to have an early night.

It wasn't entirely a lie, she didn't feel well, but Henry would assume she was in physical pain, not the emotional pain she was actually experiencing.

He sent a message right back:

Henry: Do you need food? Painkillers?

Laura: No, thanks, just sleep. You should spend some time with your mother.

CHAPTER TEN

WITH LAURA HAVING an early night, Henry had little choice but to spend it with his mother. If he cried off and took himself out she'd suspect he was trying to avoid her.

Which he probably was. Though he couldn't figure out exactly why.

He loved his mother, he enjoyed her company, but her unexpected arrival had punctured the bubble he and Laura had created in the castle over the past few weeks and he resented that.

As he showered before dinner his mind wandered. Was Laura actually unwell or did she also not want to have dinner with him and his mother?

No. Surely she knew she was more than welcome to join them. Surely Laura knew what an important part of his life she was.

She might be important, but she's also temporary.

Caroline hadn't disapproved of Laura; if anything she was overjoyed that he was dating someone. His mother's enthusiasm at finding someone in his bed that morning probably shouldn't have surprised him, but it had. Probably because he understood that his relationship with Laura would end soon but his mother did not.

Caroline had already poured herself a gin and tonic by the time he'd dressed and made his way to the living room.

'Claudia has prepared some dinner for us. It will be ready soon. Is Laura joining us?'

He shook his head. 'She's not feeling well.'

Caroline prepared him a drink as well, despite his protestations that he could fix it himself, making him feel very much the guest in the room. She handed it to him with a sigh.

'I ran into Laura this afternoon.'

Henry raised an eyebrow.

'Okay, I sought her out and asked her to join me for tea.'

Henry wanted to slap his own forehead. 'And? Do you not like her?'

'That's not it and you know it. She's lovely, but it doesn't matter what I think of her.'

His mother's opinion may not have been the most important factor in any future partner he had, but it did matter.

'She told me about her endometriosis.'

Henry's chest tightened and he took a generous mouthful of his drink.

'No one wants to see their children go through

the pain of struggling to conceive, let alone to lose a child, at any age.'

'Mum, I know. And you don't have to worry, I'm trying to put this as delicately as I can, but Laura and I have an understanding.'

Caroline shook her head. 'You're not—and never have been—the casual type. You're loyal, dedicated, dependable. All the reasons why you are a wonderful duke.'

Henry didn't understand his mother's point. The fact that he was loyal and dedicated was the very reason why he and Laura would end their relationship when she returned to London.

'Laura knows that this is short-term thing. We've spoken about it. We've been very honest with one another.'

Caroline raised an eyebrow and he felt his expression from moments before mirrored back at him.

'You don't have to worry about us. Apart from anything else, I'm not sure Laura actually wants to have children. Even if she could.'

'Have you asked her?'

'Well, not…not outright.' It seemed like a highly insensitive question to confront her with.

Caroline nodded, but didn't press. They ate dinner and made perfunctory conversation about the farm, about the fair.

When he couldn't stand it any longer he asked, 'And what else did you talk about?'

'This and that. I told her that the treatments these days are so much better than they were thirty years ago.'

'You didn't!'

'It's true, they are.'

'But that's not the point.'

He shook his head, wanted to get out of there as quickly as possible to check in on Laura, even via message if she didn't want to see him.

He could understand her staying away now. Caroline wasn't trying to send Laura away—what she was trying to do was just as bad. If not worse.

They ate in silence for a while, Henry's annoyance gradually subsided as he realised his mother wasn't trying to be unkind, she was simply coming from a different place.

'How did you both stand it?' he finally asked.

'What?'

'The pressure to have an heir. And to deal with that when you'd already lost Daniel. Didn't you ever think it wasn't to be? Didn't you ever just accept it and give up?'

'We couldn't give up. It wasn't an option.'

Yes, not having an heir wasn't an option. Not for his parents. Not for him. Or for his own children.

'But Henry, darling, we had you. And we couldn't love you more or be more proud of you.'

* * *

The week leading up to the fair was hectic. He and Laura had a few stolen moments together, though he still made his way to her cottage and her bed each evening. The pair of them had silently conceded the space of the castle to his mother while she was staying. While he was frustrated that the work on the fair took him away from the time he had left with Laura, he was downright glad of every excuse to avoid his mother. She'd never come out and said anything directly, but every look, every sigh she gave suggested she thought that if they were not planning a future together, continuing to spend time with Laura was a mistake.

But his mother was wrong. Or at least, partly wrong. Not spending time with Laura felt like the bigger mistake. Yes, it would end, yes, Laura would return to London and they would see less of one another, but cutting her out of his life completely? Impossible.

Besides, Laura knew the score. If anything, she was more focused than he was on finding him someone else to date, but even thinking about touching another woman was impossible.

Every time he walked past Natalia he wanted to wince.

Life would be simpler if he'd fallen for someone like her in the first place.

But he hadn't. How could he once SohoJane had come into his feed and Laura had walked into his life?

The morning of the fair was bright with a cool breeze that promised to subside during the day. He kissed Laura and slid out of her bed at 5:00 a.m. She groaned softly and went back to sleep.

When he saw her next, several hours later from across the main field, every breath left his body. She was at the jam and fresh strawberries stand with a woman who looked like an older version of Laura.

Laura was wearing a long floral dress; her loose hair swayed a little in the breeze. He watched as she tucked a strand behind her ear and laughed with her mother about something.

Everything else at the fair, the sounds of the cows mooing, the squeals of delighted children, the tractor roaring during a demonstration, all fell away and there was just her. Amongst the vintage cars, the skittle games and the children's rides, Laura turned and her eyes found his.

He crossed the field, taking in everything about her, anticipating the softness of her cheek against his, the bliss of holding her hand in his.

'Henry, this is amazing. I've never seen a fair like it.'

His heart expanded against his ribcage with

pride. He loved being a part of this event, being a part of the community. He loved the role he got to play in it.

'Thank you. And you must be Fiona. I am so happy to finally meet you,' he said and held out his hand. Fiona took it but also leant in to kiss him briefly on the cheek. When she pulled back she gave him a quick wink. Both her eyes sparkled.

As pleased as he genuinely was to finally meet the amazing Fiona, there were now two meddling mothers too many here today and he hoped that chance and circumstance would keep them both apart.

Fiona introduced her companion, a man named Tony, who was looking eagerly at the cider tasting.

'Are you having a good time?' Henry asked them all.

'Wonderful,' gushed Fiona. 'The fair is lovely, but I'm mostly so glad to be seeing this one again.' She put her arm around Laura.

Henry couldn't argue with her. As proud as he was of the fair, it was Laura who was the brightest part of his day.

'Let me show you all around.'

'Oh, no, we can find our way and see you later on. You two enjoy yourselves,' Fiona said.

Taking in the smells of frying food, fairy floss and fresh grass, he led Laura around to all the best sights. She licked her ice cream made with the milk from the local cows. Admired the cleverly decorated cakes and the flower displays.

'What's your favourite thing?' he asked her.

'I don't know yet. I've heard a rumour there are puppies and kittens.'

'You heard correctly.'

'Well, I'm guessing, that will be my favourite thing.'

The barn was across the field, so he took her hand and they walked through the groups of smiling people. He couldn't help but beam at everyone he knew, noticing as they noticed Laura and smiled broadly at both of them. Walking across the fair holding Laura's hand made him almost as happy as seeing the entire fair come together again successfully for another year.

'What's your favourite attraction?' she asked.

You, he thought, but said, 'The pony rides.'

'Why?'

'It's one of my earliest memories. I went on them every year and as soon as I was old enough, I'd run them.'

'How old were you?

'I think I was about eight.'

She laughed.

'What's so funny?'

'I was imagining an older teenager, not an eight-year-old!'

'I may have had some help,' he conceded, but

for as far back as he could remember he'd helped in the running of the fair in some way.

'I love all of it—it's just about my favourite day of the year. I've never missed one.'

The smile on Laura's face faded, but he wasn't sure why. The many animals would be sure to cheer anyone up. They had chicks, piglets, lambs and of course the puppies and kittens. As usual, the barnyard was one of the biggest attractions, with a line-up of people young and old waiting to see the baby animals. Henry and Laura lined up with everyone else, but when they reached the pen with the eight-week-old sheepdog pups, Annabel, who was running the barnyard, gasped. 'You didn't have to line up, Your Grace.'

Henry's cheeks warmed as the heads of the tourists turned and looked at him with wide eyes.

'He's waiting with me,' Laura said, as though that explained it.

Introductions were made and then Annabel turned to Laura, 'Would you like to hold one?'

'Am I allowed?'

'Of course.'

Annabel let Laura into the pen, where the pups circled her ankles. Annabel scooped one up and handed her to Laura.

Laura beamed and started talking softly to the pup. Henry couldn't hear exactly, but it sounded as though Laura was reassuring the pup that she was both safe and gorgeous.

'Oh, she's so lovely. They are all lovely,' Laura gushed, and Henry couldn't agree more.

She was lovely.

Love. It had so many meanings, so many possible uses. He loved his mother. He loved the annual fair. He loved the castle. He loved the taste of the vanilla ice cream from the homemade ice cream stall.

Laura was lovely and he adored her.

But did he love her?

The word 'love' was so overloaded with implications. If it was love he felt for Laura, was it the type of love that would last a lifetime? Was it the type of love to overcome everything that he would have to sacrifice to be with her?

They left the barnyard and he took her to the cider-tasting tent, no more certain about his feelings. After tasting a few varieties and choosing their favourites they took their drinks out to the shade of a nearby tree.

Henry knew it was a question that was bound to cause pain and maybe he shouldn't even ask it. But his mother's question had got him thinking. He cared about Laura and wanted to know the full extent her condition really was having on her life.

'I have a question for you, but I'm not sure if I should ask it.'

She tilted her head. 'Why not? We've always been able to be open and honest with one another, haven't we?'

They had.

'Did you want to have kids? I don't mean now. I understand that's too complicated. I mean when you were younger did you want kids?'

As suspected the question did cause pain. She grimaced.

'I guess when I was I kid I did, in the way that you do when you don't really understand what something actually involves. And now I don't really let myself think about it. I want to live pain free and besides, I'm happy with my life the way it is—I love my job, my family, my friends. I don't feel as though anything is missing from my life.'

He nodded, glad of the answer.

'I'm sorry for bringing it up, I just want to know you and know what you're thinking and feeling.'

'It's okay,' she said, sipping her drink. 'Like you said, we've always been able to be honest with one another.'

The sun had dipped below the horizon and the crowds were dispersing. A hardcore group were still enjoying the cider but the pony rides and farmyard nursery had all packed up and gone home. She watched Henry, just out of earshot, talking to a group of people. He was smiling broadly and gesturing enthusiastically.

'It's just about my favourite day of the year.'

She could feel the passion and satisfaction emanating off him.

That was when she knew she was lost. A duke, who was at home in London's boardroom, but at heart was a farmer. An animal lover. A tireless supporter of his local community.

He wanted to pass on the pony rides to his children, and not even because he was a duke, but because he was a man who longed to be a father, whether he'd admit it to her or not.

And her lack of fertility had never hurt this way before. It had always been a theoretical idea that she'd accepted—before her maternal instincts had ever kicked in she'd shut them off.

But now, she wanted children for *him*.

She wanted him to take his own kids to the pony rides, to watch them grow and take over the running of the fair and the castle as he had done.

She watched him bid goodbye to Natalia. She would make a good partner for him. She loved the estate. She would give him a brood of cherubic blond children. Laura's stomach ached, but not with a cramp. She clutched her arms around herself but sat up straight when Henry approached.

He sat down next to her with a sigh, his hair

mussed, face red maybe from exertion or sun, it was hard to say. He looked tired but content.

A little like he looked after they'd made love.

'Are you all right? Do you want to go?'

'I'm fine,' Laura lied. 'It's not a cramp. Just too much ice cream.' And too much gorgeous duke. 'I want to find my mother though.'

They located Fiona sitting at one of the tables set up near the food vans. Tony had made some friends in the cider tent and was talking to them. He seemed kind and friendly and was taking the whole, 'Please meet my daughter's boyfriend the Duke of Brighton' thing as though he met dukes every day, for which Laura was glad.

'We'll make a move shortly,' Fiona said. They were staying at a B & B not far away in the village. Laura had suggested they stay with her, but Fiona had scoffed. 'Bring my boyfriend to stay the night under your roof? I'd sooner take him to my own mother's.'

It had been lovely to see her mother and to meet Tony. Laura began to slip back into her reverie about Henry as she watched him stand again and talk to some departing stall holders.

'He's quite a man,' Fiona said, softly.

'He is.'

Laura waited for the 'but', though Fiona seemed waiting for Laura to speak next. Finally Fiona said, 'You'll never guess who I ran into.'

Laura was sure she'd never guess. Her mother knew precisely no people in this part of the world and she couldn't begin to guess which of her mother's many friends would end up at the Abneyford village fair.

'Caroline.'

'Caroline?' There was only one Caroline here Laura knew.

'The duchess, silly. She told me to call her Caroline.'

'You met? How?' Laura spluttered. *And why are you only dropping this on me now?*

'She thinks you're very impressive.'

'Yes, she's happy with my work, not with my relationship with her son.'

'I didn't get that impression at all. She says Henry is very taken by you.'

'Yes, but…that's why…'

'You told her about your endo?'

'I had to. It didn't seem fair not to, and Henry hadn't. She needs to know that Henry and I aren't serious about one another.'

'Endometriosis isn't a reason not to be serious about one another. It's obvious to everyone here today that you like each other very much.'

'But it's the reason we can't be together.'

'You know, I've watched you struggle with the condition for the past fifteen years, half your life, and do you know what has impressed me? You never give up. It might stop you for a few days, but you get back up there—you have refused to let it stop you obtaining your dreams.'

'This is different, Mum, it's not a degree or a job. It's not something I can overcome by hard work and willpower.'

'I thought you'd accepted that you probably wouldn't have kids.'

'I have. But Henry hasn't and it's different for him.'

'How is it?'

'Because he's a duke—he needs an heir or the title dies.'

'Is this what he thinks? Have you let him make his own mind up?'

'Of course—but, Mum, I'm not letting Henry risk his family's future on me.'

'Isn't he a risk worth taking? Aren't you a risk worth taking?'

Oh, if only he was. Oh, if they could both forget everything else about their lives, if she was pain free, if he didn't have a title and responsibilities to his family...then it wouldn't be a risk at all.

But they did have those things. They did live in this world, not a fantasy one and they both had issues and burdens that made living a life together impossible.

Laura shook her head, trying to find the words. She was saved by Henry's arrival.

'We don't have the final figures, but it looks as though we raised over a hundred thousand pounds.'

'Amazing. Well done. And what will the money be used for? A local charity?'

'No, actually, we usually choose an international one. We are all so lucky to live somewhere like this. This year we're donating it to Doctors Without Borders.'

Henry's attention turned fully to Laura and her heart melted under the warmth of his smile.

'I won't be too much longer. I just need to check on things at the finance office and then we can head back, if you like?'

'Great.'

'Fiona, will you and Tony join us for a nightcap?'

Fiona laughed. 'Thank you, but we've both had enough of the cider for one day.'

Henry held out his hand to her again and Fiona stood and kissed his cheek. 'It's been so nice to finally meet you. Thank you for looking after my little girl.'

Laura watched her mother and Henry share a moment and had to look away. They would have got on well together, she thought, though this was likely the last time they would ever meet.

CHAPTER ELEVEN

HENRY FOUND LAURA in her workshop. The room was unrenovated, stripped back to its original floorboards and with simple white paint on the walls, but with large windows and a view over the ruins.

The room was tidier than when he'd seen it last. Only one painting, the one she was examining, remained in the room. The significance of this was clear to him; he wished they'd had a little more time.

He half hoped she'd discovered several paintings with almost irreparable damage that would require her to stay for weeks.

'Hi there, can you give me a few more minutes?' she said when she realised he was there.

'I haven't come to hurry you. I'd just like to watch, if that's okay.'

'Of course.' She gave him one of her gentle, soft smiles. The one that did wild things to his insides and made him want to pull her into his arms and breathe her in for ever.

She was brushing the canvas with a small soft brush, soft enough to clean away dust but not damage the paint.

He watched her work, carefully, methodically. Lovingly.

He *had* to stop using that word.

It took so much effort to look after the collection of paintings, several weeks' work most years. And then there were the tapestries. The soft furnishings. And the marble statues, the ones in the garden and the ones inside. Not to mention the castle building itself. He didn't think about the effort and cost of keeping everything up too often, otherwise the scale of it would overwhelm him.

'Is everything worth preserving?' he asked after a while.

'What do you mean?'

'How do you decide what to look after and what to leave?'

'You're not just talking about the paintings, are you?'

'Paintings, tapestries, documents, historic houses.'

Dukedoms.

She took her magnifying glasses off and focused on him properly. Obviously confused by what she saw she looked away and took her gloves off as well.

Placing them down and stepping away from

the canvas she said thoughtfully. 'I guess it depends on the significance of what it is. Its historical importance. How expensive it is. How much it's loved.'

Loved.

There was that unhelpful word again. 'Yes,' he replied.

'But most of all it depends on the cost.'

'The cost?'

'Yes. You're paying me. Not everyone who owns artwork has the resources or time to look after it. It depends on what it costs to preserve something for future generations.'

The estate could afford the cost of preserving the paintings; from an economic point of view, the cost of preserving them was less than the increase in their value each year.

But preserving the title of the Duke of Brighton? Preserving his family line? What was that worth? What would that cost him?

That wasn't a mathematical equation.

Or was it?

'So some things aren't worth what it'll cost to keep them?'

'You could say that. But I think I mean, at least in my line of work, sometimes the cost of looking after the thing is more than the owner can afford.'

'But if you have the money? If you can afford to protect the thing?' he asked. Who better to ask this question of than a conservator? Someone who cared as much about preserving history as he did, if not more.

'Then I think it should be fixed. And I'm not just talking about nineteenth-century artwork, I'm talking about the environment, the forests, the oceans. All of it.'

She was right. And he realised, it wasn't about him. The castle, the title, the estates—it was bigger than him. It was there before him and would be there after him. He'd been being selfish. Too focused on himself and his own desires.

'I don't have much more to do. I'd like to get a second opinion on the Rossetti and I'll need to go back to London for that. If it's okay with you I could always come back for a day or two in a month's time, when we have those results.'

'Of course that's okay. Are you saying you'll be finished soon?'

'Yes, probably tomorrow.'

Tomorrow! 'So soon?'

'It's been six weeks.'

Had it? It seemed shorter…but also long enough for his life to change. How slippery time was when you were falling in love.

Love? Why did he keep using that word? It wasn't helpful. Particularly when he wasn't sure it was even true.

Laura tidied her tools up and brushed her hands

together. She lifted her arms up and stretched out her limbs and torso.

He took in every movement, tried to take a photo with his mind of her long limbs, the sublime look on her face as she closed her eyes as she extended her arms as high as they would go above her head, entirely unaware of how glorious she was.

She shook her body out, the signal she'd shifted her mind from work to play and gave him a different smile now, broad and sparkly. A definite gleam in her eyes. Wordlessly, they reached for one another's hands.

He led her through the quiet rooms of the castle, then through the back corridors to his rooms, the family apartments thankfully empty since his mother and her friends had departed. It was theirs again, for one more night.

He tried to push that thought from his mind as he placed a trail of kisses from her delicious lips, past her soft ear lobes and along the silky skin of her neck and collarbone. He tried not to think of it as she shivered under his touch, sighed against him or groaned when his lips finally reached her hard nipples.

He tried not to think of it when she took him in her hands and softly, expertly brought him just to the brink. But it was a hard balance to maintain, needing to forget that this was their last night together while also wanting to ensure he memorised every kiss, every shiver. They both held on and on, in silent but unanimous agreement that this was it. That this must be it. They both knew it and they were both keeping one another honest; if he started to waver, she'd remind him of what he really wanted.

They were lucky in a way, to know it was the last time. He'd never known before. Couples didn't usually, did they. They'd make love like it was any other time, not knowing or even thinking it would be the last time.

But they both knew.

They held on, they went over every inch of one another's bodies, committing each pore to memory. Each sigh. As she moved on top of him with her eyes closed he watched her, felt himself inside her, breathed her in, held on for as long as he could. When release came it wasn't a relief—ecstasy was mixed inevitably with heartbreak.

No. He must enjoy each moment. Make the most of it. They'd always known they had an expiry date. He could hardly complain now when this had been the deal he'd made with his heart all along.

'That was nice,' Laura murmured into his neck.

He could only give a hum in agreement, any other words would give his thoughts away and he didn't want her to know that his heart was breaking.

That would only complicate matters. He knew enough about Laura to know that he'd only make her feel worse if he confessed to all the feelings that were currently rolling through his body like an out-of-control wave. Not to mention he'd been the one to suggest the friends who have sex arrangement in the first place. He'd sound like he was reneging on their deal.

And he wasn't. He knew she would return to London. He knew this must be their last night together. But that still didn't stop his heart from slowly cracking and quietly disintegrating as he held her.

Henry knew it would be impossible to search for sleep when he wanted to spend every available minute looking at her, at the way her thick lashes rested against her cheek as she slept, at the creamy clear skin of her shoulders that tasted slightly different to the creamy white skin of her breasts, at how, feeling her skin against his own, breathing her in. Filling his lungs with as much of her as possible in the hope that something would be left to sustain him through the weeks, months and years that would follow.

Despite his resolution, when the sun started to make itself known above the horizon, the exhaustion from his all-night vigil caught up with him and he finally gave in to his body's demands for rest.

When he woke a few hours later, disoriented, the sun bright, Laura was sitting, dressed, on the edge of his bed.

'We need to talk, don't you think?' she said.

'What if...?' Laura started talking before she'd even managed to articulate the thought.

What if I tried. What if I stopped taking the drugs? What if we gave it a year? What if we saw the best fertility experts in the country?

Was that a crazy thought? Was she ready? Was he? Even though in some ways she felt as if she'd known him for ever, in reality they'd only met properly a little over a month ago.

She took a deep breath. She'd wonder for ever what might have happened if she stayed silent.

'What if...and I'm not saying we should, I'm just asking, what would it look like if we tried?'

Henry was silent for a long while before finally pulling himself up and rubbing his eyes. She regretted not letting him wake properly, at least give him some caffeine before dropping all of this on him. The thoughts had started after the talk with her mother, even, if she were honest, after the talk with Caroline.

Henry rubbed his eyes, still trying to focus. Or delaying.

She stood. This was probably a big mistake.

'Laura, wait. Please just give me a moment.'

'Yes.'

She went to the kitchen, put the kettle on for her, turned the coffee machine on for him. When he came out of his room a few minutes later he was wearing shorts and a T-shirt, but he'd accessorised with a grim look.

She placed two fresh mugs on the table and sat. He sat too.

'What would it look like if we tried to have a baby?'

'Now?'

The doubt crept back. 'Yes, I mean, I know it's soon. Forget I said anything.'

He reached for her hand, ignoring the coffee. 'For starters, we'd need to get married,' he said. 'Because any heir would need to be born in wedlock.'

She nodded. She'd kind of forgotten that part. Marrying Henry would be the easiest thing in the world.

'And we'd try to have a baby. You'd get advice from your doctor, we'd get all the best help we could.'

Laura was already lucky enough to have an excellent doctor. Her chances of conceiving in Dr Healy's care were as good as they could be.

'And if it doesn't work?' he whispered.

She looked down, tried not to cry. *This* was what they really needed to be considering. The possibility that after years of pain they'd have nothing to show for it. The pain and disappointment could rip them apart, but if it didn't, if it made them closer then what? He'd be childless.

He'll leave you for someone else. He'll have time. Laura would have spent years of her life possibly in pain, but she'd spend them with Henry. That wasn't nothing.

She projected forward five or ten years. She'd be disappointed because she'd allowed herself to get her hopes up; Henry would be disappointed and trying not to be bitter. They could be even more heartbroken than they both were now. Or worse, they'd be bitter and resentful.

Either way they'd mostly likely be in a worse position than they were now.

'You're right, I'm being silly. It's just the fact that I'm about to leave and I'm confused.'

'No, Laura. I like that we talk about this. I love that we can talk openly and honestly with one another. Don't ever stop doing that.'

They could both picture what might happen if she stayed, likely slightly different images of the projected mess, but the outcome was the same.

'Laura, this is important. I care about you too much to put you through that. I don't want you to go through what my mother went through. But most of all, I don't think I can stand to keep seeing you in pain, month after month. I don't want that for you.'

'There's no need to make excuses, I do understand.'

'What on earth do you mean?'

'I'm strong, Henry, I can make up my own mind about my body.'

'I'm not...' Henry's face reddened. 'I didn't mean you couldn't. I'm trying to tell you, maybe awkwardly, that I care about you. I care about you so much that I don't want to put you through the same pain.'

Laura's skull seemed to tighten and press on her brain. She closed her eyes, but the pain filled her head, impairing her thoughts.

'It's exactly what I said. I don't want to see you in pain. And I don't want to see you disappointed.'

And then she understood because it was the same for her. She wasn't going to stay and she wasn't going to put either of them through this because she cared for him as well. She cared for him too much to let him give up everything he'd been born to do.

It was silly of her to suggest it, but she wanted him to know that she would be prepared to make those sacrifices for him.

'I know what your mother went through after losing Daniel and then those years of treatment

SWIPE RIGHT FOR MR. PERFECT

and I just want you to know that I'd be prepared to try. I'd be prepared to do that for you.'

'Oh, Laura. Is that what this is about? I know you care about me. But it's different for you. Mum wasn't in the same kind of pain that you are.'

Embarrassingly, she started to taste salt. She took a gulp of tea but as soon as she looked back to Henry and deep into his blue eyes, so full of soul and worry, the taste came back. She spoke quickly to get the words out.

'I'd be prepared to do all that, but I'm not going to let you do it. We both know it has to be like this. Even if I don't have the operation, the chances of me conceiving are so low. Miracle level low. The chances of me carrying a baby to term are lower too.'

He passed her a tissue and she wiped her nose.

'I don't want to put you through any of it, Laura. It wouldn't be fair.'

He was right, but she added, 'Henry, it wouldn't be fair to either of us. And it's okay to say that. I won't do that to you or your family. It would not be fair to anyone.'

He nodded and she knew they were making the decision together, they were talking like rational adults. Then why was it so goddamn hard?

Because they were both calm, and rational. And because they both knew.

It wasn't a screaming match. Even her tears

were calm. Soft, silent and so, so calm. The only outward sign that this was actually it, that it was actually over was the clump of wet tissues in her hand.

She held her stomach. Not because of the familiar pain that had wracked her every month for the past fifteen years, but a different pain. It was the pain of her heart tearing apart, not her ovaries.

Laura stood, but before Henry could as well, she touched his shoulder, leant down and kissed his cheek.

'Let's just remember last night. I don't think I could stand it if you hugged me now.'

Laura was using every ounce of bravery in her to walk out that door. If he held her again she knew she wouldn't be brave enough.

CHAPTER TWELVE

'WHAT ARE YOU doing here?'

'I came to check on you.'

Henry had walked into his kitchen and found his mother sitting at the table flicking through a magazine.

Henry couldn't remember the last time his mother had called by to 'check on' him. She hadn't made such a gesture when his father had died, or when he'd broken up with Beatrice. It wasn't that she was uncaring, she just seemed to know that he was coping both those times.

Unlike now.

No. He was coping. He was getting up each day. Eating. Well, mostly. Showering. Every other day at least. Sleeping? Well, no one was perfect.

Not that his mother should have any idea about what he'd been up to. He'd been keeping to himself, keeping busy with work. He hadn't wanted to impose himself on anyone. And it had barely even been a week.

'Why? I'm fine.'

Caroline said nothing but glanced at his attire. His pyjamas. It was midday on a Monday.

'I worked late last night. I slept in.'

'I hear you've been keeping quite irregular hours.'

He had a traitor in his midst. Did Claudia work for him or his mother?

She worked for his mother. Who was he kidding.

'I got engrossed in some research about liver fluke in sheep and I just kept going. I'm keeping the place running. I'll get dressed soon enough.'

Caroline pulled a face, and shook her head before going to the coffee machine. Henry sat at the table while she brewed him a cup. The sun had been easing its way above the horizon by the time he fell asleep. Since Laura left he'd felt as though he was suffering some kind of bizarre jet lag that only seemed to get worse as the days wore on, rather than better.

But it would get better. It would. He'd been heartbroken before and survived.

But then he'd had a plan. And a future that stretched on for years.

Now what did he have?

It felt like he had an impossible to-do list.

1. Get over Laura
2. Find someone else to fall madly in love

*with, preferably before I get too old to actu-
ally hold the child I can't even dream of having with someone else*

The thought of loving someone else turned his
heart to stone.

Caroline passed him the coffee.

'I'm sorry, I didn't realise you loved her so
much.'

'I...' He opened his mouth to deny it or to dis-
miss it but that was impossible. 'I'll get over her.
I just need some time. But Mum, please, I'm not
ready to start dating again. Please just give me
some time.'

'Was it her decision?'

That was blunt. 'Is that relevant?'

'I'm not sure.'

'It was both of ours.' Was it? Their last conversation was now a jumble in his head, but he'd
been utterly convinced they were doing the right
thing. It was only now that he wasn't sure. 'But
mostly me. I guess.'

She regarded him now. He knew he didn't look
like a man who was happy with his decision.

'Because of her condition?'

He nodded. 'Yes.'

Caroline sighed.

'I thought you'd be happy,' he said.

'Why would you think that?'

'Because now I can find someone else who doesn't have fertility issues, because now I can produce an heir.'

Caroline looked at the ceiling and sighed deeply. Then she took his face in her hands. 'Never, never think that I want you to be unhappy. Never think that I want you to be heartbroken.'

Henry looked into his mother's face. The last time she'd held him like this had been years ago.

'Sweetheart, I'm so sorry. I wish there was something I could do.'

'There's no way around it, though is there? You know it—I know it.'

'How do I know it?'

'Losing Daniel.'

'It's not the same thing.'

He was filled with shame and spoke quickly, 'No, I didn't mean that it was like losing a child.'

'No, you misunderstand me. Losing Daniel was awful, as was losing your father. But I didn't have a choice. Those were things that happened that I had to live with. *You* have a choice.'

'I don't, not really. I don't want Laura to suffer. I don't want her to be in pain and I don't want to put her through years of procedures and attempts to have a child that we just may never be able to have.'

'But why do you have to do that?'

'Why do you think?' Had she forgotten the

small detail of needing an heir? Had she forgotten all the sacrifices she'd made herself to secure the inheritance?

'Do you mean for the title?'

'Of course that's what I mean. What else?'

'Henry, darling, I didn't go through all that just to provide your father with an heir. We did it because we wanted a child. We did it because the pain of losing Daniel was so much, because I couldn't stand the thought of no longer being someone's mother. The title wasn't the only reason. It was about us still wanting to be parents. Do you understand?'

Henry shook his head. All he understood was that his mother appeared to be changing the story he'd been told all his life.

'You were born to inherit the title. You were born because your brother died.'

That was what he'd been told for as long as he could remember. By his father. His mother. Everyone.

'I was born to inherit the title. I was born because Daniel died.'

'Yes, but that doesn't mean…' Caroline shook her head. 'You are more important than a tradition. You are more important than this.' She waved her hands around the room.

'No. I'm not. This *is* me. I am the dukedom, I am Abney Castle.'

She shook her head. 'No, dear, no. Those are a job and possessions—you are more than that.'

'You went through half a dozen rounds of IVF, you nearly died giving birth to me. You sacrificed so much.'

'But that was my choice. I'm not expecting you to do the same thing. I'm certainly not expecting Laura to.'

Not outright, he wanted to say. But Laura knew as well as he did, that the expectation to produce an heir would be on her. It would be on both of them.

'I'd never ask her to go through that.'

He'd never let her. Besides, once she had the hysterectomy, it was a moot point.

'We wouldn't be able to have our own children.'

'And that's okay. If you love her, be with her.'

Henry shook his head.

His entire life he'd been taught that the family title was the most important thing. More important than him.

'We did it for the title, yes, but most of all, we wanted you. Don't ever forget that. I don't regret having you for a moment and I'd do it all again in a heartbeat.'

Henry finished the dregs of his coffee and stood.

She couldn't change history with a few assertions. No one could. Neither of them could. He was born to be the duke. He was born because his brother died. They were facts, pure and simple, and no one could change that.

Fiona had been very gentle since Laura had arrived back in London. She'd left her alone to begin with but this evening had suggested they meet for an early dinner since the weather was so nice.

Laura was throwing herself into work, into London, into anything that wasn't Henry. Of course each time she looked at a painting one of the ones at Abney Castle came back into her mind. And then, so did he.

It was the right decision. She'd been brave. As brave as she could be. She hadn't been brave enough to message him. Or hug him goodbye. But she'd been brave enough to pack her car and drive back to London and to pick up her life again.

Fiona was already seated at a table outside at one of their favourite Italian restaurants. She stood when she saw Laura and hugged her as though they hadn't seen one another in months.

'How have you been feeling?'

'Sad.' Awful, distracted, tired.

'I know that. I meant pain wise.'

'Oh.' Laura had to think. It had been weeks since her last attack. It had been that time Henry had found her in her cottage. It had lasted a few days but after that she'd been fine. Maybe the operation had worked better then she'd first thought. She'd been so distracted with a different kind of pain, the one in her heart, she hadn't realised that remarkably, her pelvic pain had been manageable. She'd had twinges here and there but nothing to stop her from working.

Or from any other activities.

The irony of it made her laugh. If she hadn't been so well, she wouldn't have spent so much time with Henry, wouldn't have grown so close to him. Wouldn't be struggling to be parted from him.

'Are you going to stay in touch?'

'It's just too hard.'

'For you?'

'For everyone. For me, yes, but him too. And for the woman he does marry.'

Fiona frowned. 'What makes you think he's going to up and marry someone else?'

'Because he has to.'

'You think he will marry someone he doesn't love?'

'No. But he will find someone to love.'

'Not when he's in love with you.'

'He's not. He can't be.'

'Saying it isn't so doesn't make it not true.'

'He can't love me because that wasn't the plan.'

'And was you falling for him the plan?'

'No, but it doesn't matter if my heart is broken.'

Fiona took her daughter's hands and leant across the table. 'Now, you listen to me. Your heart is every bit as important as his. You have just as much right to happiness.'

Laura shook her head,

'I can't believe you're saying this, Laura.'

'I just mean that I always knew the outcome of this in a way he didn't. But I know I'm worthy of love and happiness, of course I do.'

'Do you?'

'I do.'

'Then let him love you.'

'That's not what this is about.'

'Isn't it? Have you given him the choice to love you or did you just rule it out for him?'

Had she? She didn't know. It was so hard to re-member, when all that came to her mind was his touch, his smell, how she felt so good with him, how she was powerless to stop the attraction be-tween them. How it seemed so inevitable.

I won't do that to you or your family. I'm not going to let you do it.'

It didn't matter whose choice it had been, the decision had been made. Henry hadn't stopped her, hadn't contacted her. He knew it was for the best even if her heart was having a hard time ac-cepting it.

Henry trudged up the hill, through the wild-flowers. Often he strode up there, determined, focused. But today he could only be said to be dragging his feet. He was going up to the mausoleum, not because he wanted to, but because he *had* to. Because the answer would be up there. He had to go up there to remind himself why he was putting himself through this torture.

He was doing it for his family. For the twelve dukes who held the title before him, not to mention their wives. He was doing this for his family. For his father, his late brother.

And most of all for his mother.

'We did it for the title, yes, but most of all, we wanted you. Don't ever forget that. I don't regret having you for a moment and I'd do it all again in a heartbeat.'

Surely she didn't really mean for him to give up everything she and his father had done to have him, to raise him? Surely his ancestors didn't think he should be knowingly and willingly putting an end to the family line. To a four-hundred-year-old tradition?

He reached the classical-style building and unlocked the door. The last time he'd been in here was with Laura, all those weeks ago.

The night after he'd shared the story of Daniel they'd made love for the first time. He'd told her they were friends, but even then he knew that their relationship had changed for ever.

I love her.

He loved her then and he loved her now.

His knees buckled and he fell onto the marble bench in the middle of the room and held his face in his hands.

He loved Laura.

It was only because he'd been denying the truth to himself that it was actually a revelation. He'd loved her since that day. He'd probably loved her well before that, but admitting it had been impossible. Except now that he had uttered those words, now that he had to face the truth, what would he do?

He couldn't marry her. She wouldn't have him for starters—she'd made it clear that she wasn't going to let him give up everything for her, even if he'd wanted to.

So he had to love her and be apart from her. That wasn't the end of the world, he told himself. People did that all the time and they still got up every day and ate food and went to work.

They found other people.

But did they? Really?

How would it be fair to any women he might marry if he still loved Laura?

And what if, though it was unthinkable now, his pain faded enough for him to let someone else in and what if for some reason they didn't have children? Did that mean his life wasn't worthwhile? Far from it. Everything he had done and built would still exist. His life would still have meaning.

'You are more important than a tradition. You are more important than this.'

He looked up and over at the graves. First his father. His wonderful strong, devoted father who had lived a life of duty, dedicating himself to his family and the estate.

Daniel, the brother he'd never known but desperately wanted to, first as a child and especially now. Daniel could have given him advice. Except he couldn't. Because if Daniel had been here then Henry would not be. There was no version of reality where he and Daniel would both exist.

Henry looked to the bust of the ninth duke, who was buried across the room from his wife. Had he been honourable? Henry doubted it. Was it worth giving up Henry's own chance of happiness for that particular duke?

The fourth and fifth dukes? They'd dabbled in slavery and the tobacco trade. Not worthy of celebration, let alone emulation.

But there was the sixth duke, who had built this building for his beloved wife, where they chose to spend eternity together. By all accounts they were honourable.

Henry pulled himself up and walked over to his father's and brother's graves.

Honour, faith, love.

Was it more honourable to lead a loveless life of duty? Was that really what honour was about? Was that really what his ancestors had lived for?

Was it honourable to turn your back on the person you really loved just because tradition demanded it? Required it?

You were born to inherit the title.

You were born because your brother died.

Maybe those two things were separate? And maybe they didn't have to define him. Yes, both those things were true, but that didn't mean he had to sacrifice everything. Maybe his mother was right—it had been her choice to have him. And maybe, just maybe, by focusing too much on the first word in the epitaph, he'd neglected to consider the other two.

Faith.

Love.

Was he free to make his own choices? Was Laura?

And if so, would she still have him?

CHAPTER THIRTEEN

IT WAS FIVE o'clock in the evening, but the sun was still bright and high. Laura couldn't decide if she would work another hour or leave with her colleagues who were slowly pouring out the door for the day.

Since returning to London she'd been working late most nights, mostly because being alone in her apartment in the evening was excruciating. If she worked late and got home even later then it was like the evening didn't happen. Like she didn't miss having dinner with Henry, talking about their days.

Like she didn't miss messaging FarmerDan.

For the first time in months she had no Dan. And no Henry either.

At the thought of his names, her phone lit up with a notification.

@FarmerDan: How was your day?

Laura's heart rate went from resting to tachycardic in a second. They hadn't spoken about not contacting one another, but she'd assumed it was implied. Maybe in several years' time, when the shape of their lives had shaken out, then maybe they could catch up with one another, but not a week later. That was too soon. Her phone shook in her hands and another message appeared.

@FarmerDan: I know you probably weren't expecting to hear from me, but I'm in London and I'd like to see you. It's important.

It's important.
He wouldn't just ask to meet if it were not important. He wouldn't say it was important if it were not.

His mother? Had she damaged one of the paintings and not realised? What could it be? Every scenario she could think of was bad news.

@SohoJane: I'm just finishing work now.

@FarmerDan: I'm one block away.

While willing her heart rate to remain calm, she grabbed her bag and left her office as though she was evacuating the building. She saw him as soon as she exited the door. He was ten paces down the street, facing the opposite direction, giving her a moment to look at his back, his broad shoulders, his hair, neat for once. London hair, not farm hair. Her body felt like it was breaking in half.

Would it ever stop being this hard?

By the time he'd turned and noticed her she was wondering if it wouldn't be easier just to turn and flee. They walked towards one another, slowly, but inevitably.

Should they hug? Kiss?

Henry leant down and pressed one cheek briefly against hers, like an air kiss with a relative, not an old lover. Her heart sank.

'What happened? Is everything okay?' she asked.

'I hope so.'

'Is anything wrong?'

He looked around. 'Where can we talk? Is there a pub or a cafe nearby?'

Something was wrong. Yet, he didn't look devastated, tired and washed out to be sure, but there was something buoyant about his demeanour.

A thought hit her like a stab.

He's met someone.

Surely not, she told herself. It had barely been a week.

But if he did what she'd suggested and got back on the app then...

She didn't want to know. She wanted to turn and run home and never think of Henry Weston ever again.

Henry wouldn't do that to you.

She nodded to the park across the road. He found a bench and they sat.

'What's the matter? What's wrong?'

'Everything.'

'Everything?'

'Yes, everything. I've made a mistake. About us.'

Her foolish, hopeful heart started up its dance again.

'Oh.'

'I can't do it—I can't stop thinking about you.'

She wanted to fling herself into his arms, but sat on her hands instead.

'Do you just think you've made a mistake because we miss one another? That will happen—that's to be expected.'

Henry took her right forearm in his hand and she let him tug it from under her to hold her hand in his. Warm and earnest, his grip was pleading.

'No. It's more than that. I don't want to get over you. I don't want anyone else. I only want you for the rest of my life and I'm so sorry I didn't say that last week.'

She looked down. 'I want to be with you too, but I'm not going to make you happy. I won't make you give it all up. I won't let you resent me.'

'I've been thinking a lot over the past few

weeks. I've been thinking of nothing much else really. I've decided I hate it.'

'What?'

'My title, my inheritance. In a way I never have before. I hate that I'm powerless to change it. It's my identity…but then again, is it? I will always be the Duke of Brighton, for as long as I live. I'll run the estates, help the village. And when I die, the estates can be left to anyone or anything I choose. I can't take it with me. No matter what.'

'But the title? It'll be lost.'

'Not lost. Just no longer living. It doesn't mean that everything that happened before loses its meaning. It doesn't take away anything my father did, or my mother, or my great-grandfather. It also doesn't fix all the bad things some of my other ancestors did.'

'Are you saying you don't mind if we can't have children?'

'I'm saying, unless you want to, I don't think we should try. I think we should agree on that now. That way we both understand and agree what our life will be like now. No one will get their hopes up, or be resentful if it doesn't happen.'

She couldn't disagree, but was he sure? What if he changed his mind? What if…?

'I want to show you something else.'

He opened a window on his phone and showed her a calendar entry.

'We met with the National Trust this afternoon. My mother and me. We had an initial meeting, putting the process in train, for them to eventually take over the management of the castle. You need to understand—I'm not risking the chance to have an heir. I want to give it up. Now. Once and for all. I propose to bequeath the castle to the National Trust.'

'You're giving up your castle? For me?'

'I'm not looking at it like that. I'm making sure that it's preserved for ever by people who also want that. Besides, who's to say I wouldn't have irresponsible kids who'd run it into the ground anyway? It's too much responsibility for one person. Too much of a burden. And my mother agrees.'

'She does?'

'We had a good talk. It was her idea actually.'

'But what about Daniel? Everything she went through?'

'She says that was her decision, she never intended that I would feel obligated to carry on anything, unless I wanted to.'

'But don't you? Want to?'

'I thought I did, but I realise I hadn't thought about it properly at all. I took so many things for granted. I don't want to have an heir if it means I can't have you. You are more important. Happiness is more important.'

He was prepared to give it all up for her. Not just risk it, but give it up.

It was like a fog was lifting from her thoughts and suddenly everything she saw looked different.

'Your mother knows? She's really okay with it.'

He nodded. 'Yes. She… I was wrong about her. I was wrong about a few things.'

'What will you do?'

'I'm not giving it up just yet. I'll still have plenty to do.'

She almost believed him. Almost. Bequeathing the castle to a trust, she understood that. Letting the title die, she understood that too. But there was something else, something so many people wanted with all their very being.

'But you won't have kids. You won't be a father.' Then she added quietly, 'Will I be enough for you?'

'You are enough for me and always will be. You have to believe that.'

'I do. It was never about me not feeling good enough for you. It was about not wanting to disappoint you or your family.'

'You could never disappoint me. I love you, every part of you.'

Love.

That word.

She opened her mouth to say it back but the words caught. It was too much.

'That's why we met with the National Trust. I don't want you to be in pain and I don't want you to feel pressure. I want you to know that I've made the decision. I love you, Laura.'

That word again…

'I love you too, Henry.' This time when the words flowed it was like breathing.

And then it was real. He moved forward quickly, as though she would take it back, and kissed her.

I love you… I love you…

The words swam in her thoughts as he pulled her closer.

Henry drew back and screwed up his face. 'Will you still love me if I don't have a castle?'

She laughed. 'I didn't fall in love with a duke. I fell in love with a farmer wrestling a calf. I fell in love with a tennis tragic. I fell in love with a man who loves his family. And pony rides.'

'I fell in love with a woman on a dating app who said she was taking a break from dating.'

It was true, she'd fallen in love with the man who messaged her each evening just to ask about her day. Who always listened, who was always there.

'So, tell me, how was your day?' she said. 'Best thing? Worst thing?'

He smiled and kissed her.

EPILOGUE

Dr Healy's rooms were familiar, but the mood Laura took in with her today was not. She felt centred, determined, and for the first time in a very long time very, very sure.

The feeling of calmness might also have had something to do with the fact that Henry was with her. She always came alone to these appointments, but he'd insisted on coming today. Going to tell your gynaecologist that you were ready for your hysterectomy was a big deal, even if the decision had already been made.

She had made her peace with it, as had Henry. They were both looking forward to spending the rest of their lives together. He loved her as she was, and she did not feel any pressure to put her body through something to fulfil anyone's idea of what sort of wife she should be.

Laura had relocated to Gloucestershire but had been given a consulting role with her firm. She would still do occasional work in London, but most of her work would be around the country.

She and Henry had nascent plans for their own business, helping the owners of other listed properties to preserve the properties and the paintings.

They had shifted their focus from Abney Castle to English Heritage as a whole and it was invigorating. They were embracing the idea of handing the property over to the National Trust when the time was right. They both felt that even though one door may have closed, many more other doors had opened.

They were also both looking forward to a long and languorous honeymoon in Italy once Laura had recovered from her surgery. The future was bright.

Laura's name was called, and Henry squeezed her hand.

Dr Healy smiled at Laura and Henry when they walked into the consulting room together. 'This is Henry, my fiancé,' Laura said.

'Congratulations, have a seat.'

They all sat, and the doctor began. 'How have your symptoms been lately?'

'It's been mixed, I suppose. The month immediately after the laparoscopy was one of the worst yet.'

'And after that?'

'I've had some respite actually, but I know it's only a matter of time.'

'When was your last period?'

Laura thought.

'It's been…'

'Ten weeks?' guessed Dr Healy.

'Er…gosh… Well, possibly, yes.' Her cycles were never regular, but ten weeks did seem unusually long. She must be mistaken. With everything that had gone on with Henry she'd been very distracted.

She'd been experiencing discomfort, though it had been different. Higher up. Not as severe.

She'd been tired too, but that wasn't unusual.

'I've got your recent blood results here. They are…interesting.'

'Interesting? How?'

'You prepared for a scan? You've drunk enough water?'

Laura had a full bladder; it was hardly her first pelvic ultrasound. She nodded and went behind the curtain, took off her pants and put on the gown. Dr Healy would see the extent of the adhesions.

'May I stay?' Henry asked.

'Of course,' Laura and the doctor said.

Dr Healy directed Henry to the best place to stand. He picked up Laura's hand and squeezed it again.

'By the way, I've had some spotting between periods for a while now. I assume that is because of the medication?'

'That could've been due to ovulation.'

'I thought the medication was meant to stop that?'

'It may have, but not necessarily. We've only started you on a low dose to begin with.'

'What does that mean?' Laura was suddenly concerned. Was there something else wrong with her as well?

'Let's just see what the ultrasound says.'

The gel was cold on her stomach, the pressing of the probe hurt her full bladder, but Laura took her mind elsewhere. To Henry. Waking up in his arms this morning in Brighton House, to the life they would have together.

'Ah, yes.' Dr Healy was smiling. 'It's as I thought. Now, I know this isn't what you wanted to hear, but you may want to rethink the hyster-ectomy.'

'I've made up my mind. I know there are many things I have to sign—'

'That's not why. There's something you need to know. Do you see this?'

Laura was familiar with what her ovaries and uterus looked like, but the picture in the screen was slightly different. She saw something puls-ing and drew in a sharp breath.

Surely not.

'Do you know what you're looking at there?' the doctor asked.

'I'm new at this,' Henry said. 'I think I'm going to need you to explain it to me.'

'It's consistent with your blood results. I'd say you're about twelve weeks in and there's a heart-beat.'

'A heart what?'

'A heartbeat. Laura, you're pregnant.'

Henry dropped her hand but only to step over to the monitor to get a closer look.

'You're sure?' he asked. She was glad he'd asked that question. She didn't think she was capable of speaking.

Dr Healy laughed. 'As sure as I can ever be. Your dates match, the blood results are clear, but that heartbeat doesn't lie.'

'How?' Laura gushed.

'The usual way, I expect.' Dr Healy laughed. 'Were you using contraception?'

They looked at one another and shook their heads.

'There's always a chance. And the first few months after a laparoscopy can sometimes be the most fertile, as they appear to have been for you. I hope this is a good surprise?'

'It's certainly a surprise,' Henry said.

'Shall I leave you two a moment? I think this isn't what you both were prepared for.'

Prepared? She'd been preparing for a hysterectomy, a wedding and a honeymoon in Italy. Not a baby.

'I'm not prepared at all.' Then a horrible thought. 'But I drank alcohol and coffee. I didn't take vitamins.'

'Relax, it's still early days. It's very common for women not to realise. The baby will be fine. Though we should keep a reasonably close eye on you, given your history.'

They left the rooms in a daze, not knowing what to do first. Laura led Henry to the same bench she'd sat on back in the depths of winter just after she'd received a different type of news.

'How are you?'

'Shocked. I don't know what to think…it's not something I ever allowed myself to even dream of.' Her baby. Their baby. 'I'm going to have to get up to speed very quickly.'

Henry laughed. 'We have nine months.'

'Not even! Six, according to the doctor.'

'It is ages away.'

'But I don't know anything!'

He laughed again. 'You think both our mothers are not going to want to be closely involved?'

'Oh, my.' The thought of telling them both made her head swim. But she knew she'd have all the support and love she needed from their mothers. And Henry.

She glanced around the square; the grass was green and the trees heavy with leaves.

'Back in the winter, I sat here and told you I couldn't date. Dr Healy had just told me there was very little chance I'd ever have children.'

'Very little is still some.'

'Yes, but realistically. Oh, Henry, I said you didn't need a condom. I wouldn't have suggested we forget the condoms if I'd known.'

'And thank goodness you did.' Henry was as shocked as she was, but she could tell by the brightness in his blue eyes that he was overjoyed.

'But… I…' She wasn't yet sure how she felt. Or even if the news had sunk in.

'Laura, this is the best news I think I've ever had…but how do you feel about it, really?'

'I'm still shocked and scared. No, I'm terrified.'

Henry's face creased. 'But are you unhappy?'

'No, I don't think so. I'm amazed. But also terrified. Henry, I never even let myself dream about this.'

It was going to take some thinking about, some planning. But Henry was with her and would be all the way.

'How are *you* feeling?' she asked him.

'All of the above. Laura, like I told you, I love you no matter what. This is a wonderful surprise, but it also isn't what I was expecting either. We'll have to move the wedding date up. How do you feel about a small register office wedding?'

'I'd marry you anywhere. Anytime.'

'We could do a bigger thing, later, if you like?'

She smiled. She didn't need a big wedding. Just being with Henry was enough.

'I'll marry you as many times as you like,' he said.

'Oh, Henry,' she laughed. 'It's too ridiculous. I never even let myself imagine this.'

'Try now.'

She closed her eyes and in a flash she saw a child's face. It had dark hair, like hers, but Henry's eyes.

She wasn't just having a baby; she was having Henry's baby.

He squeezed her hand again. 'This child will be able to make its own mind up about what it does with its life. There's only one thing I want it to inherit.'

'What?' she asked.

'Your eyes.'

She laughed and shook her head. 'Absolutely not. No way. I think they should have yours.'

* * * * *

If you enjoyed this story, check out
these other great reads
from Justine Lewis

The Billionaire's Plus-One Deal
Breaking the Best Friend Rule
Beauty and the Playboy Prince
Back in the Greek Tycoon's World

All available now!

HARLEQUIN
Reader Service

Enjoyed your book?

Try the perfect subscription for Romance readers and get more great books like this delivered right to your door.

See why over 10+ million readers have tried Harlequin Reader Service.

Start with a Free Welcome Collection with free books and a gift—valued over $20.

Choose any series in print or ebook. See website for details and order today:

TryReaderService.com/subscriptions

RSBPA24R